The Unquiet Night

The Unquiet Night

Patricia Carlon

Published by
Soho Press, Inc.
853 Broadway
New York, NY 10003

Printed in the United States of America

Library of Congress Cataloging-in-Publication Data

Carlon, Patricia, 1927–
The unquiet night / Patricia Carlon.
p. cm.
ISBN 1-56947-194-0 (alk. paper)
I. Title.

JUL 0 6 2000

PR9619.3.C37 U57 2000
823—dc21   99-048518

10 9 8 7 6 5 4 3 2 1

CHAPTER ONE

HE hadn't meant her to die. It was a cruel trick of fate that she had; that in spite of all his efforts her head, with its stiffly lacquered dark hair, lolled helplessly when he tried to move her, and that the half open dark eyes gazed, slyly-bright, into nothingness. He had thought at first she was shamming; taunting him some more; reminding him of things he wanted to forget, not remembering that it was unlikely that she should even know about his past. He had shaken her till his arms had ached, but it hadn't altered anything. The slyly-bright eyes didn't open and her slack red mouth refused to utter so much as a protest.

He urged her, "You're fooling, aren't you? Say it's all right. You made me crook and if I got rough you asked for it, didn't you? You did, didn't you?"

She wouldn't answer.

In the end he got slowly to his feet, standing there, suddenly trembling hands thrust deep into the sheepskin-lined pockets of the leather jacket.

Her black stockings had a small hole in the left leg, just above the knee. He could see the white flesh circled there, stark and bare, where the red skirt had ridden up a little. There was a long streak of dirt across the red of the skirt, too, and her black twinset was crumpled and twisted round her thin body. He didn't dare look at her face any more. His gaze flickered up and over the stiffly lacquered hair. It seemed someway indecent to him that in spite of her crumpled, soiled appearance the hair was still tightly correct, as though she was waiting for another date; as though as soon as he turned his back she would get up and go away

Deep in his dazed brain he knew that he had to move and get right away from her and from the lake and the carpeting red leaves on which she lay. He had to go right away before he was found there and they locked him up for what had happened.

But he hadn't meant her to die. He said it aloud, his voice a harsh whimpering croak in the stillness of the place. He hadn't meant her to die. It was her own fault it had happened. He hadn't meant it to happen that way at all.

He had been out for fun that Sunday. He had seen her waiting at the bus stop and had known, right away, that she wasn't waiting for any bus. You could tell it about the girls like her. They never stood right at the yellow stop—just a little to one side of it, so they could pretend, when a bus did come along, that they were just there waiting to meet a bloke or some other sheila, who was coming along any minute.

What they were waiting for in reality was a bloke in some car who would pull in and give them the time of day, parrying words with them while their calculating gaze ran over the car and its owner, deciding just what they were worth for a date.

He'd seen it happen dozens of times. He had tried it himself, only it wasn't often one of them accepted his offer of a lift and a coke or coffee somewhere. He had only the motor-scooter and scooters didn't rate highly with the sort of girl who stood just to one side of a bus stop. Their bright eyes were on the lookout for cars, the bigger, the shinier, the better, or bright new bikes. A scooter was a small thing to them.

But he'd chanced his luck that day when he had seen her waiting. The street had been quite deserted except for himself and the girl and a ginger dog harrying a flea, and she had looked so gay and bright in the red skirt, with the red bow stuck in the mass of upswept black hair—gay and bright against the grey contrast of the quiet, dull-skyed Sunday.

He'd pulled up beside her and said, "Well?" and after a minute the blue-shadowed lids of her eyes had blinked down over her calculating stare.

6

She had asked, "What do you want?" but when he had laughed at the question and told her to come off it, she had suddenly laughed too. It had been easy after that. He'd been pleased, with a warm happiness under the leather jacket, right where her slim hands had pressed as she had held on to him as the scooter had travelled towards the lake. He'd even whistled a little, thinking of the hours ahead.

But everything had turned sour later on, when she'd realised he just wanted to talk; to tell her about all his ideas — all the jumble that pressed and burned in his brain and to which no-one would ever listen. She had said at first, "Well, you're a queer one, aren't you?" and tried to break across his talk, but he hadn't let her and after a while the red mouth had turned down. She had even started to hum, to sing half under her breath, the drone of it hiding the words, annoying him.

When he had told her to be quiet and listen she had retorted flatly, "Who says I got to? I didn't come to sit and freeze and listen to you. You're silly anyway."

He'd been angry then, and she'd grown angry in turn. She had called him silly again and told him he ought to be locked up and blind fury had taken over his actions. He'd wanted only to shut out the words: to stop the taunting, when he had caught her by her slim throat.

At first she had looked astonished, then angry, then her expression had changed to fear and panic and pain. He could remember, looking down at her, the way it had kept changing till suddenly there had been only blankness left.

But he hadn't meant her to die.

In sudden terrified revulsion he tugged at her, managing, his breath coming in sobbing gasps, to drag her to the edge of the incline overlooking the grey, undisturbed waters of the lake. With a last shove he pushed her and stood watching, his mouth open in heaving gulps of air, as she rolled slowly downwards into the water.

She didn't cause an upheaval or loud splashing. The red of

her skirt simply mingled with the red reflections of the flame trees in the grey water, the black of her twinset and hair looking like shadows across it.

He was half sobbing as he stumbled away. The leaves that carpeted the ground under the trees seemed to cling to his boots, as though they were trying to hold him, stopping him getting away. He went blundering through them, heavy-footed only one urgent thought now with him—to get back to the motor-scooter and get right away, back along the rutted dirt road to the highway and the town.

Then he saw them.

He saw the child first and stopped dead, standing there with his hands thrust again into the sheepskin-lined pockets of his jacket, thought turning from the urgency that pleaded with him to get away, to the knowledge that he hadn't been alone in the reserve.

He stood staring, taking it all in in a slow sweep of his blue eyes, from left to right. He could see the trees, some of them bare-branched, some of them still leafed in flame and orange, the gums still green in the foliage they would hold all through the Australian winter. And below them the child running, dancing.

She was wearing a brown skirt and yellow coat—the skirts of it twirling out round her as she moved, her plump arms outthrust as she twirled on the toes of her brown strapped shoes. Her pigtails moved too—two thin out-thrusts tied with brown ribbons at the sides of her round solemn face. She was quite intent on what she was doing, unaware of him as he stood there, and after a moment he took a step backwards.

Then he saw the woman.

She had the same light brown hair as the child, but hers hung straight, brushed back from her pale forehead, with a brief upflick at the ends of it. She was wearing green slacks, her long legs curled slightly under her.

And she was watching him.

8

He turned slowly, meeting her eyes. His wits couldn't cope with the unexpectedness of seeing them there. He'd heard nothing, yet all the time she and he had been . . . his thoughts baulked and stopped.

He said, whispered, "Hello."

. . .

Rachel had been feeling pleasantly relaxed and at peace. She never minded coping with nine-year-old Ann. She had said so that morning to Deidre, when her sister-in-law had rung and gone into one of the breathlessly involved explanations that seemed to have no ending and which were particularly her own.

She had propped herself comfortably against the cushions of the blue couch, tucked the phone under her chin and gone on painting her nails, waiting for Deidre to come to the point. When that had happened she had said, "Of course. I don't mind. Ann's never any trouble."

She had refrained from adding that in her private opinion her niece was a small edition of her solicitor father, Roger Penghill, who had rarely, when he and Rachel had shared a nursery together, summoned together the necessary devilment of character to get into even the mildest of trouble, and had added, "I'll collect her in an hour and we'll picnic. I'll trot her back this evening. Just keep calm."

"It's all very well . . ." the heated protest had made Rachel laugh.

She had said gently, "I know. I don't realise the stresses and strains of married life. Let's thank God for it and not get on to my on-the-shelf condition. I'll trot her back this evening as promised, or wait on . . . do you want me to rally round this evening as well ? How long is this shindig of yours going to last?"

"That's the rub, I simply don't know," Deidre had wailed. "But tonight's all right, because we were meaning to go out anyway, and I've got to cancel that now and it's going to be frantically awkward because Wilma always does something elaborate and being Sunday she'll have fixed most of it yesterday probably and then there'll be just the two of them to eat it . . . oh and the dog of course . . . but you couldn't feed a dog on duck say, without feeling guilty I should think . . . but anyway I'd arranged for Sandy to come in."

"The Purple Peril?" Rachel had murmured, contemplating her gleaming nails with satisfaction.

"What? Oh well, she is rather, isn't she? All those horrible purple clothes and that make up . . . but she *is* responsible. I wouldn't pay her four shillings an hour otherwise and she's coming this evening, so if you'll bring Ann back and wait around till Sandy comes up I'll be eternally grateful."

Even with that settled it had taken Deidre another ten minutes before she was satisfied everything was fully agreed. Rachel had already ceased to listen long before she replaced the receiver. She was simply sitting there debating what to wear and where to go. She had decided on green slacks and the thick russet pullover that was warm if not exactly beautiful, and was pondering the thought of a lake picnic by the time Deidre hung up.

As she had known would be the case, Ann was no trouble. The child agreed to the lake and to suggestions of what they would eat with a calm affability and sunny smile and had made only one request of her own—that they should stop off and buy a new box of crayons for her drawing-book.

She had settled down happily in the reserve to draw the autumn scene, leaving Rachel to her own thoughts and the soft music of the low-tuned radio beside them. She had hardly noticed Ann leave the book finally and go dancing away under the trees. She was quiet, absorbed in the faint music, the slow flutter of leaves from the flame trees and the tingle of slowly chilling air on her face.

It was the last fact that was penetrating her thoughts when she saw him. She was beginning to wonder if they had better return home; whether it was going to rain; whether they could find a warmer spot in the deserted reserve, when she realised there was someone else there. Someone besides Ann.

When she looked round he was watching the child, so intently, her own gaze turned in quick anxiety to look at the dancing figure. Reassured that nothing was wrong there, she looked back at him, taking in the bulky-looking body—a bulk not altogether due to the heavy leather coat, she was sure, but to fat as well; the butter-yellow hair flopping over his forehead; the youth of his half averted face.

Then he turned, looking full at her with round blue eyes. He said dully, after a moment, "Hello."

"Why, hello to you, too," she said briefly.

She thought, now that she could see him full-face, that he wasn't as young as she had thought him at first. Twenty-one or two, or even a bit older, she reflected, then wondered why she bothered to notice. She was suddenly angry that he had broken into her pleasantly peaceful mood. She hoped he didn't intend to stay around, talking inanities, or even in an immature way, trying to pick her up. She was sure, gazing at him, that anything he tried in that line would have immaturity about it. Then she reflected, half in amusement, half in relief, that Ann's presence was a guarantee against him even trying. One didn't, however gauche, try to pick up a woman who was towing a child around.

But abruptly she found herself wishing he would say something more. His stare was becoming disconcerting, his rigidity a little unnerving. And then she thought in amazement, "Why, he's sweating. On a day like this. At the tail end of autumn. In a place like this. How odd." Because she could see the fine sheen of moisture on his pale face.

Even while half of her was still listening to the music, she was thinking of the oddness of it, wondering if he had been running, even of what he might be wearing under the thick leather jacket.

Then abruptly he made a strange choked sound deep in his throat and went stumbling away, his blundering feet sending little spirals of disturbed leaves into the air behind him. Uneasiness touched her, the uneasiness that went with an oddity unexplained. She went on sitting there, the music forgotten now, reflecting on his sudden appearance, his dulled voice, his stare, and the blundering departure, and then moisture touched her face, gently at first, then stingingly on her bare skin.

She called "Ann!" and saw the child was already moving. She called again, "The car—run for it!" and grabbed at the radio, the rug and the picnic basket, hugging them all awkwardly to her slim body as she tried to run after the child.

There was dampness on her shoulders and face and she could smell the tang of dampness in her hair, too, when she scrambled into the car at last, leaning over to drop the things onto the back seat.

She was turning the ignition key when she asked suddenly, "Ann, did you see that man?"

The child looked back blankly, her round face solemn.

"It doesn't matter," Rachel told her and then so suddenly that she actually laughed, she thought of the reason for his rigidity, his brief speech, his blundering departure. He had meant to try to pick her up of course, and then he had seen Ann dancing. Disappointment had dulled his wits for a little and then he had blundered off in angry impatience.

It would be something, she reflected in wicked amusement, to tell to Deidre. Dear, but at times thoroughly exasperating Deidre, who regarded her sister-in-law's twenty-nine-year-old spinsterhood as an affront to nature and common-sense.

"I might be fading rapidly," she would declaim dramatically, "but I'm not beyond getting a pass or two . . ."

She said, still half laughing, "It's no use stopping out in the rain. We'll go home—play cards if you like or anything else you fancy. Will that do?"

·   ·   ·

The black fear that had settled down on to his mind couldn't be washed away by the rain trickling down his face. He had made no move to start the scooter. When it had finally dawned on him what he'd done he had been incapable of doing anything. All he could think of was that the woman had seen him. Not only that, she had looked at him full-face. For a minute. Two minutes maybe. He couldn't think straight of how long it had been. But she'd gazed full at him.

As soon—as soon as she was missed and searched for and found—the woman would describe him. Wouldn't she? He wondered frantically how he had looked to her—if his shaking hands had been in her sight—if she'd seen in his face all the horror he had felt.

But she hadn't cried out, he reasoned desperately. She hadn't looked anything except faintly annoyed at him being there, so he couldn't have looked odd, could he?

But she'd seen him. That was the point he had to face up to. Soon she was going to be able to talk to the police and describe him. Wasn't she? They'd know it was today the girl had disappeared and they'd want to know who'd been by the lake and they'd learn about him. *All* about him. He could smell the sourness of sweating fear along with the damp of his clothes. They'd take him away. Lock him up . . .

He could hear the thin voice again, "You're a queer one. All that talk's plain silly. Belt it up, silly. You ought t'be locked up, silly."

·   ·   ·

They were talking of the rain as they drove away from the reserve. They laid bets with each other that it would stop just as suddenly as it had started, by the time they reached the first turn-off on the long, rutted dirt road that led from the backwater of the lake to the highway and the town. When they reached the turn-off that led to one of the farms it was still raining and they laid another bet that the second turn-off would see it finished; then by the time they reached the goat's head sign that led to the farm where the two women kept goats.

It was still pouring by the time they looked up at the white sign. There was a fine mist blowing towards them into the bargain. Only the few flame trees along the road gave any colour to the greyness and shabbiness of the scene.

Rachel said on impulse, "What would you say if we went up to the farm and asked to see the baby kids? The women couldn't be busy out on the farm in the middle of this weariness, so they wouldn't really mind us coming, would they? Think not, Ann?"

.   .   .

He didn't know what to do. He sat in the coffee-room, as far from the other people in the place as possible. That meant he was a good way from the oil heater and the pleasant circle of warmth near it, but he didn't think even Hades could have warmed him. He was cold with a chill that he knew had little to do with the late autumn day, or the pouring rain outside, or the wetness of his clothes and hair.

He ordered coffee, but when it came he made no move to drink it. Only when the steam rising from the cup blurred his vision did he warm his hands round the china. He drank thirstily then, bending his head to the cup, barely raising the latter from the saucer. It was poor stuff, a fact that irked his already hard-pinched nerves.

If he hadn't been so intent, so determined, to avoid notice, he would have protested in a spate of the angry, sarcastic words that flowed easily from his lips when he suspected he wasn't being given what he was entitled to. Over the years, since he had learned his physical limitations, he had perfected the defence of words both to shield himself and to bludgeon a path for himself.

But words wouldn't help him now. He began shivering again and in a thick rasping voice he called for more coffee, forgetting for a minute that he didn't want attention drawn to

14

himself. But no-one looked round and the age-wearied eyes of the woman in charge of the coffee urn were interested only in his shilling and not in himself.

He drank the second cup hardly pausing for breath. The warmth seemed to seep into his mind, releasing the frozen rigidity of thoughts that had centred on his stupidity in letting himself be seen.

Deliberately he turned his mind back to the lake and what had happened there with the girl. Rose, that was her name. *Had* been her name. That fleeting reminder, piercing his recollection, reminding him she was dead, almost unnerved him all over again.

Her name had been Rose. She'd told him that. And she was dead. And the woman had seen him and could describe him. They were facts. So what was he going to do?

Make it seem that Rose had died somewhere else? Some place a long way from where he'd been seen?

He knew after a little that it wasn't going to work out. He remembered the way Rose had rolled over into the water, becoming a part of it. Even if he could reach her and manage to drag her out, what was going to happen then? To shift her he'd need transport. Not the scooter. That was useless. He'd need a car and he didn't have one.

There were ways of getting one, his thoughts reminded and impatiently he disposed of one idea after the other. Even if he could trust to his small knowledge of cars to use one he'd need to show a licence to hire one and if he knocked one off . . .

He knew that wouldn't work. It would only need someone who knew the car to see *him* in it, or even the police getting the word of it had been lifted and stopping him . . .

It would be worse than having the woman speak out. If he was caught with Rose he couldn't deny a thing. Could he? And after all him being by the lake wasn't to say he'd done Rose in. Was it? He could always deny everything and let them try and prove he'd done it. After all he'd never been connected with Rose in any way, had he? And maybe the woman hadn't really got a look at him. Had she? Maybe she'd even forgotten him right then?

He was too frightened to believe in it. He was sure she'd remember. Just so soon as she heard about Rose she'd think of her outing. Wouldn't she? And remember him. And once the police had him . . .

And if he dared take a car and chance his luck to shift Rose, where could he take her? He thought of the gently undulating farmlands that stretched away into the distance for miles, trying to convince himself there were plenty of places — in little gulleys, in out of the way spots, where he could leave her.

But he knew what would happen when she was missed. The whole district, farmers, townsfolk, even people just passing through the district, would be out searching. It had happened before. They'd find her sooner or later. They'd still know how she died. Wouldn't they?

But just because he'd strangled a dog once in a raging temper — that wasn't to prove anything, was it? They couldn't prove anything against him if Rose was found a long way away — where it didn't matter that he had been in the reserve that day. In fact, if the woman said he'd been there the day Rose disappeared, that would be *fine*. Wouldn't it? They'd have to believe he had been by the lake that day, not miles out in the country, on some deserted farmland, on some . . .

The sweet relief that had risen warmly in his throat was gone as swiftly as it had come.

He was remembering the time of the previous search. It had been a boy then. A boy who'd drowned in the lake and they'd proved he'd drowned there and nowhere else — though he himself had never understood why they had gone to all the trouble to prove it when the boy had been fished out right there — but it had been in the paper. He remembered poring over it and thinking what a waste of time it had all been, proving the water of the lake had something . . . some special content . . .

he groped desperately in memory. Lime, was it? Yes, lime perhaps. Something that made it distinct from all the other rivers and waters around. There'd been water in his lungs. In his body. In his sodden soggy clothes. They'd known he had died in the lake.

And was there lake water now in Rose's body? Drenched into her clothes? To tell the world as soon as she was found that she'd been in the lake? That she'd died in the reserve?

She'd be found quickly. It couldn't happen any way else. They'd know where she'd died however far he took her. So it wasn't any good. So soon as they knew and the woman spoke out he'd be done for.

But what if he buried her? So deep they could never find her again and then . . .

He moved painfully in his seat, anger rising in him, a more bitter anger because for once his tongue couldn't cover his physical disabilities. He lifted his left hand from the table, staring at it unblinkingly, thinking of the arm under the leather jacket—the thin, bent arm that he couldn't lift above his head even. The arm had condemned him long ago to the sort of job where one stood up behind a counter and "yes-madammed" a pack of fool women who didn't know their husband's size in collars, yet expected him to know it without blinking. A good chance his sister Ivy had called the job, and a fat lot she knew about it. But she'd made him take it. She'd threatened what she'd do if he didn't take it and stick to it, and she knew too much for him to buck . . . not about the dog and the warder in the home. The police knew about those. They'd put him in a home for six months because of the dog, and then there'd been the warder. And afterwards . . . there were other things Ivy knew about.

And she wasn't going to keep quiet if she knew about Rose and the woman who'd seen him. She'd told him often enough, "One more time, Mart. Just once and that's your finish."

But there wasn't any strength in his arm for digging a grave. And that left what?

Gropingly he thought of weighting her and letting her sink out of sight into the bottom of the lake. As slowly he groped it into consciousness, it was gone, because the lake would be the first place anyone would think of when she was reported missing. They'd think of an accident first. They'd drag the bottom of the lake and they'd find her. They'd still know when she had died and how. And the woman would still be waiting to describe him.

But what if she wasn't? What if she wasn't there at all? If she could never say a word?

CHAPTER TWO

FOR the first time there was pleasure for him in the fact that it was raining. There was even pleasure in the cold soddenness of his clothes and hair, because the discomfort was a reminder that the weather was giving him time. While the downpour kept on no-one was likely to go near the lake and see where the shadows became something darker and more solid and where the red of the reflected flame trees was blurred into something else.

He wondered how long it would be before Rose was missed. Not that day he was sure. And maybe not that night. Her type kept their own hours and their own counsel about where they'd been and what they had done. But say there was in her house and her life some folk who couldn't rest till the household was in — who sat and worried till the last set of footsteps came down the hall and the last bedroom door closed? Then maybe Rose would be missed late at night. But even so they . . . the person awake and waiting for her . . . wouldn't ring the police straight off. Would they? They'd wait for a long time. And even then the police wouldn't head out in the dark for the lake. Would they? It wouldn't be till some time in the morning that someone went near the lake, or after she had been reported missing and the police got moving and went there . . .

And if she wasn't missed till the morning itself, when her empty bed was found? He could picture quite easily what would happen. The sort of people who'd bred and reared and cared for a Rose didn't run straight to the police. There'd be endless talk and strong cups of tea and the neighbours called in for advice before the final step was taken. It might be well into the afternoon even before someone finally got the lake dragged.

The eagerness he had put into the conjecture died away. After all, what did it matter. Time alone wasn't going to fix things. Time was only given him to think and to work out what to do. To try and find a way out. Nothing was altered for all the hope that she wouldn't be found for twenty-four hours. In the end she'd still be found and they'd know how she died and where and when.

He was back to that and suddenly there was nothing in his mind except the idea of flight. His feet shuffled into movement and his body began to tense and shape itself into the action of rising and then he was still again.

Because flight wasn't going to help.

He didn't have any money. Nothing worth while. And there wouldn't be much at home, even if he could get it while Ivy's back was turned. And it was Sunday. No way of getting at the forty or fifty pounds there was in his bank account. No way till ten in the morning. And it might be too late by then.

Even if he lit out where was he going? Once the woman described him and they went to Ivy and heard all she had to tell, the hunt would be on for him. They'd mention his arm. Wouldn't they? Put photos of him in the papers—Ivy had plenty of snaps of him to hand out. And then what? There wouldn't be a place in the country safe enough to hide him. Even if he someway changed his looks there was still his arm. What was he going to live on as well? You had to have references, his frantic mind warned, for a job behind a counter. Employers weren't going to let any come-by-chance get their fingers into the till. The only jobs he might find without a reference were pick and shovel, casual, a few days here and a few more there, type. And there'd be hardly one of them didn't need two good arms.

Everything came back to the woman.

But maybe she wouldn't come forward. What if she didn't say anything? What if she *couldn't* come forward? If she *couldn't* say anything?

·　　　·　　　·

He was back to that and he didn't want to be. He had refused before to dwell on the point. Now he had to. Because there was nothing else to think about. If she couldn't speak out no-one could point a finger at him. Not even Ivy. There'd be no-one to say he had ever been near the lake or Rose that day. The police would guess, well enough, when they learned what sort Rose was, how it had happened—a pick-up and a fight. But there'd be nothing to point his own way. If the woman only kept quiet.

Slowly the panicky excitement died down again. He was back in another dead-end. Wherever the woman was now she was safe from him. She could be any point of the compass. Perhaps she belonged to the town, on one of the farms, or further away. If he had ever seen her before—if she had ever walked through the doorway of Spencers, Men's Outfitters— and told him the size of her husband's shirts, he didn't remember her. Or the kid. He'd never seen either. She was just a face, just a long slim body, just a wide mouth, just a pair of what . . . grey, blue? . . . he couldn't remember . . . just a pair of eyes that had looked him over, just a voice that had uttered a few words, then gone out of his life.

But she could send him to prison. A stranger, who'd touched his life for a minute and yet she could send him to prison.

The injustice of it was a tight knot in his throat. He called for coffee again and when the woman brought it he grabbed at the cup, a little of the dark greasy liquid slopping into the thick white saucer. Only when the cup was empty was he conscious that the woman was still there beside him, hugging her orange cardigan round her thick-waisted body.

"What is it?" he asked dully at last. He wondered if she'd been talking at him and expecting an answer; finding something strange about him, something to remember. The thought brought panic welling sickly back into his throat.

Her voice was deep, not unpleasing. "Didn't they teach you in the school you went to that the pleasures of life got to be paid for? That's another shilling, son." She sounded amused as he gaped dully at her and she urged, "Come along, wakey, there's the boy."

"A shilling," he repeated and his fingers fumbled in the wetness of cloth.

She said, "Lordy, you're wet. Why don't you sit closer to the heater, son? You'll steam, but that's better than courting pneumonia over here."

He shook his head, putting the shilling on the red formica top between them. He was suddenly eager, desperate to get away. He moved towards the door of the place jerkily, his gaze unseeing till it rested on the white clock above the door. The hands were pointing to eight minutes past four.

•　　　•　　　•

For once Ann's placidity was thrown aside. Her voice had taken on a note of shrill whining that was as unattractive as the day outside the car windows.

"I wanted to draw the little goats," the whine protested for the seventh time.

"You can draw from memory. Be sensible, Ann!" Rachel's tone was sharp. Sharper than she had intended. It's the mean weather getting into my very bones, she thought impatiently. "Be sensible, sweet," her tone became cajoling. "By now your drawing-book will be sodden pulp. You wouldn't want it if it was handed to you. Even if we go back I'd be hard put to say just whereabouts we stopped off, and we're not . . . either of us . . . going running around in this deluge looking for a drawing-book. We'll buy another if we can find some place open. That's the best I can do about it. I'm sorry and you're desolate and the weather's horrible and our day's ruined, but let's not have tears about it all. Please, honey."

"I wanted to draw the little goats." The words were long drawn out, whining again.

"In a minute," Rachel took her time about lighting a cigarette, blowing out the match and putting it neatly into the dashboard ashtray, "I shall draw *you*. As a mean little devil, with horns instead of pigtails."

Relievedly she knew she had won. The faint, quickly snuffed out, giggle told her so. She went on speaking lightly, teasingly, as she turned the car towards the highway and the town. She didn't think again of the lake and the forgotten drawing-book.

      •   •   •

"Is that you, Mart?"

For an instant fury trembled on his tongue, then was lost in a mumbled, "Who else?" as Ivy Deeford came out into the dark little hall. Her soft, green-wool clad figure bulked large in it, her butter-yellow hair a frizzed halo round her plump white face.

She said, "You're wet."

"So's all outdoors."

"You shouldn't be standing around in your wet things like that." Her tone was still placid. She moved sideways so that he could angle past her, but she followed him down the dark hall to the little back bedroom with its window overlooking the long narrow backyard of the place. He turned towards the window, his back rebuffing her, his mind willing her to go away, but she followed him in and he had to turn because there was a flame tree right outside his window. How'd he come to forget that? When the branches of it tap-tapped against the glass on nights of high wind, when he'd lain there in the early morning lately and seen the slow flutter of the red leaves falling?

He couldn't watch it now because it reminded him of the lake and the red reflection in the water, blurring.

He said, his voice high and cracking, "If you'll only run along I can get myself changed."

The placidity of her white face and soft voice didn't change as she said, "I was only going to suggest a rum and milk, Mart. You'd like that, wouldn't you now?"

Her solicitude billowed over him smotheringly. He was

23

reminded of times when he'd been small and she, fifteen years older, and plump even then, had held him close to her, his face burrowed in her fleshy body. But the reminder and the solicitude held no comfort for him. He was afraid of her simply because she knew all about him. Because if the police came and told her about Rose and the woman seeing him where Rose had died she was going to talk.

He said huskily, "There's no time. I got to get changed again and go on out."

"Why?"

He knew she wasn't going to shift till her curiosity was satisfied, but he couldn't think of any excuse to give her.

After a minute she pointed out, "If you go out again you'll get sopping, and . . ."

"I'll wear a mac. Don't be a fool, Ivy." He hunched his back to her again, avoiding looking towards the window, beginning to unzip the front of the leather jacket. "I . . . I met up with someone and got an invite to a party. You don't expect me to say 'no' just because of a bit of rain, do you? As though I'm a kid that'll melt and get a runny nose because I'm venturing out in the wet? Or are you aiming on keeping me by the fire with a ducky mug of cocoa and a nice boiled egg?"

She stood stolidly impassive under the sudden flail of words. At length she said, still placid, "There's no need to get in a temper, Mart." Then suddenly she shot out, so suddenly that he jumped, "What are you trying to hide from me?"

"Hide . . . ?" he gulped.

"When you start in ranting you're always trying to hide something. What's happened you don't want me to know about?"

Fright cleared his wits enough so that he didn't fall into the trap of trying to deny anything was wrong, giving her the excuse to upbraid him for lying and a further excuse for her to go on talking and delaying him.

He shrugged at her, "I had a bit of a spill with the scooter.

24

There's no damage and no call for you to go on about it."

He knew she was turning the statement over in her mind, trying to pick flaws in it. Then she nodded, beginning at last to move out of the doorway.

She threw over her shoulder, "I still think you ought to settle for a rum and milk and stay by the fire, but you've got to please yourself."

When he was dressed again, in the same boots pulled up over the cuffs of jeans, with a heavy pullover dragged down over his hips and a black oilskin over everything, he took down the white crash helmet from the top of the corner cupboard. It had been Ivy's purchase, a gift for his last birthday, and a possession he loathed. Now it was a means of hiding his hair and shadowing his features.

Ivy was in the kitchen when he went in, sitting flat-footed by the table, the Sunday papers propped up in front of her against a flowered milk jug, a glass of the rum and milk he had refused beside her. The lights had been switched on against the shadows outside and her steel-rimmed spectacles were caught into two dazzling sparkling circles so that he couldn't see her eyes as he asked, "Have you got any coppers?" Forestalling her question he added, "I want to make a couple of calls."

"There's probably some in the rice caddy. You can look." She shot the question at him as he was getting the pink and gold caddy off the shelf, so that he nearly dropped it against the white enamelled sink beneath.

"Where'd you get to be as wet as you were?"

"What?" He swung round on her. "Where'd I . . . oh, I went out with a couple of chaps to . . . out in the open. We got caught."

"Down by the lake you mean? It must've been bitter cold."

His face was bent over the open caddy, his fingers scrabbling among the coins inside.

All he could think of was that she mustn't be allowed to go on imagining him at the lake. He blurted out, "I didn't say that. I meant out . . . out a long way. Passed the farms. One've us had a gun. We were going to . . ."

He stopped, unable to go on and then was wildly glad . . . so wildly glad it was difficult not to start laughing with relief. At first he had thought he was getting into a worse mess by lying. Now he knew he had hit on the very thing to keep her from thinking of him near the lake. He saw the souring of her mouth and grinned. She loathed guns, detested shooting. The very fact that he had admited to her he'd been doing what she detested would make her think he'd told her the truth.

Now when she heard about Rose she would never connect him up with it. Not unless she knew, if the woman talked, that he had definitely been near the lake. Because he'd never been interested in girls. Had he? Not as girls. Only as someone to listen to him talk and none of them bothered. It was a sore point with him. "Why don't you get a nice girl friend, Mart?" she'd ask over and over. It was the same in the shop with old Spencer saying benignly, "You know, Deeford, marriage settles a young man, and a good wife can help you get on."

So Ivy wasn't going to think of him being with Rose's sort. She was picturing him and would go on picturing him out beyond the farms with a gun, shooting birds. She'd never connect him up with Rose unless the woman talked.

His expression tightened as he shoved the coins into the pocket of the oilskin. He was sick with fright again. He told himself that he had to find her. And finding didn't mean he had to do anything to her. Did it? Not unless he was sure she would remember him. He had only to let her look at him again, and if he saw recognition in her face . . . he only had to find out, didn't he? If she didn't recognise him he was safe, wasn't he?

He got out of the place without having to answer any more questions. Ivy was still mouthing the rum and milk with the distasteful knowledge of his stated doings of the day, her tongue grimly silent.

He was whistling as he started the scooter through the downpour. Only when the red of a call-box loomed up through the greyness of the rest of the world did he pull in to a stop. He pulled open the door of it and went into the tobacco-scented, stale smell of the box, wishing it hadn't been painted red, that it hadn't turned into another reminder of the flame trees and the red of Rose's skirt.

The directory was tattered and dog-eared and two of the pages were stuck in the fond embrace of chewing-gum. One of them had to be the page he needed. It took him two sweating, cursing minutes before his penknife delicately loosened the sheets and he could find the name.

But when he had dialled the number there was only silence.

·   ·   ·

He went on waiting, because there was nothing else he could think of to do. He had no other hope he could work out of finding the woman.

The burst of hope that had come to him in the coffee-shop when the woman had demanded his shilling was his sole idea.

"Didn't they," she'd mocked, "teach you in the school you went to that the pleasures of life got to be paid for?"

And he'd thought of school. The dusty country playground and the tall, drought-sickened gums; the smell of dust seeping in through the wire-screened open windows together with the shrill sound of cicadas; the sour smell of over-hot youth that filled the room and the flick-flick of tossing plaits on the girl at the desk in front of him.

And he'd thought of the child, with her thin twists of plaits sticking out each side her round face. He had thought of her in the town school and he had known there was one chance for him of finding the woman.

He'd worked it all out in the journey home, with the rain cold on his face. He'd pictured himself at the phone, dialling

27

Hilda Thatcher's number, hearing her voice, making some excuse to find out the name of the child; telling himself over and over that there wouldn't be many small girls with light brown hair. Would there? And Miss Thatcher would know their names. Wouldn't she? Miss Thatcher with her wide beaming smile and her pleasant, "My father prefers the plain white shirts," had become suddenly a life-line to him.

He wondered, as he waited, his hand slippery with cold sweat about the black phone, if she would recognise his voice. He didn't want her to do that. There wasn't any danger in her knowing, he reassured himself, but he didn't want her to know. He didn't want his name ever to be connected with the child and the woman by the slightest thread.

So when her voice came, hurried, breathless in its, "Hello, hello there," he deepened his own.

But the smooth professional manner was still there, the deference that old Spencer insisted an employee of the shop should use, when he asked, "Is that Miss Thatcher? I'm sorry, Miss Thatcher, calling you on a Sunday . . ."

He was sure she was smiling the wide beaming smile that was as professional as his own smooth voice, when she broke in, "Don't think anything about it. I wasn't doing a thing except sleeping," and she chuckled, as though to reassure her caller that she wasn't in the slightest degree annoyed at having the sleep broken; at having been called, slipperless, her hair disordered, to the shrilling phone.

"I'm sorry," he said humbly. "It's this way, Miss Thatcher —I'm trying to get the name of a little girl. About nine she would be. Plump and with two brown pigtails. She left a parcel, Miss Thatcher. In my shop yesterday. And she's never been back. Would you know her, Miss Thatcher? A little girl about nine. Plump and with two brown pigtails. Light brown her hair would be."

It was an effort to stop talking; to keep himself from repeating it over and over, louder and louder, in an effort to make her

28

see how important, how desperate it was that he find the child, but finally he was silent, waiting.

"Well . . . there aren't many have plaits now. They're out of fashion. Such a shame I always think. You wouldn't be speaking of the little Swan girl, would you? Judith? She lives on Acacia Way. And there's Lynette English. She's twelve of course, but so small for her age."

"It might be Lynette. I'm sorry for troubling you, but if you know the address, Miss Thatcher?"

"Somewhere in Fielding Street I think. Yes, it might well be Lynette. It wouldn't be Shirley because she's a red-head. You did say brown hair, didn't you? But of course," her tone was bright, surprised, and pleased because she had thought of a way to help, "you don't have to worry a word about it. I'll simply ask at assembly in the morning as to which of them has been so forgetful and Lynette or Judith can come round in the lunch hour . . ."

"Why, that's fine," he tried to sound as pleased as her own voice. "Just fine, Miss Thatcher."

He replaced the receiver in the middle of her quick, "Who is this calling?"

He went on standing there for a long minute, wondering if there was danger in what he had done; if her questions at school assembly in the morning would start people wondering. He couldn't see that it would. The girls would deny leaving anything, anywhere, and that would be that. Miss Thatcher might be puzzled for a little while. Then she'd forget. There'd be other things for her to dwell on. School work and town gossip and her aged father and things . . . like Rose's disappearance.

Angrily, impatiently he grabbed at the directory again. There was no-one called English in the book. He'd have to find the number some other way. He didn't waste time on the point. He turned up the name of Swan. There were four entries. Two of them were business firms and one was a farm. The other listed a number on Acacia Way.

He tried fitting the name of Swan to the remembrance of the pale-faced woman in the green slacks, but he couldn't. To him she was still simply the woman. He continued standing in the box, out of the rain, planning what to do next.

· · ·

The number on Acacia Way had been in the name of B. K. Swan. Not Mrs. So that meant there was a husband, or some male relative. The tiny entry didn't tell him if there were other relatives, aunts and uncles and grandparents, and more children. And he had to see the woman alone. His one lead was that the woman and child had been alone by the lake. On a grey, cold day. It looked as though they'd had nothing else to do, no-one else to consider. It could mean there was a husband and he was simply away. It didn't look as though there were other children. Or they'd have been there by the lake too. Wouldn't they?

If the husband was away there would be a time when the child had gone to bed and the woman was alone. Wouldn't there? And if she wasn't . . . there had to be some way he could get her out of the house. A phone-call maybe, he planned desperately. A call from some neighbour. What neighbours did she have? He could maybe find out by searching through the directory. He could ring her and maybe plead sickness on the part of the neighbour, asking her to come and help. Or even . . . he thought suddenly of Ivy one evening long before her old dog had died. The brute was always getting lost and getting Ivy in a panic. She'd gone to neighbour after neighbour asking them to search under their houses, in out-sheds . . . he could maybe ring the woman and tell her he was a neighbour and a dog was lost, asking her to go out and search. It would depend on what her place was like — if there were out-buildings, places where he could wait, where they could face one another alone, and then . . .

He told himself desperately that it was foolish to go on thinking that way. Hadn't he worked out that he had to just

30

see her face to face again because after all she mightn't recognise him?

He told himself, leaving the box, that that was all he was going to do. He was going to walk up to the house and say, he was selling . . . something or other. Ask to see her. Then if she recognised him . . .

Then he knew that wasn't going to work. She'd be suspicious of him saying he was selling door to door on a Sunday. If she recognised him she'd be more surprised still and if there was anyone else in the place she'd be going back inside and saying, "Look, this is the strangest thing—I saw a man by the lake today and he's just been at the door. Selling, he says. And he hasn't even a sample case." Because he didn't have one, did he? But he could be taking a survey . . . a market survey, of the sort Ivy was always complaining about, saying the people always came when she was busy. But he knew that wouldn't work either. If the woman recognised him she'd comment on it to whoever was in the place, and mention seeing him before and later on, when Rose was found, when the woman wasn't there to talk, they'd remember about him wouldn't they? And she might have described him into the bargain to the person there in the house with her . . .

So he didn't dare do it.

He had to find out where she lived and wait till dark. That was all. And get her out in the dark alone.

CHAPTER THREE

"IT'S not as good as my other book." Ann's straight-lipped mouth was straighter than ever in that mutinous moment. "My other book had better paper—this is *shiny* paper."

"Draw shiny things," Rachel told her lightly. "Draw stars and planets and angels and little shiny-coated goats. Draw yourself with a shiny Monday-morning face, ready for school."

She had switched on the top bar of the electric fire, turned on the electric light and drawn the green curtains over the wide windows, but the room still looked cold. It was the effect of so much brown and green, Rachel thought impatiently. She had a sudden longing to rip down the green curtains and replace them with warm gold, and tear off the brown upholstery that Deidre and Roger had considered a sensible buy years before and replace it with autumn colours to shine in the light. She wondered suddenly how Deidre and Roger would react to the suggestion being made that she give them a set of loose covers, some cushions and curtains as a birthday present to Deidre. It wouldn't be expensive, she went on planning. Not too expensive anyway.

But Roger, bless him, she thought ruefully, would violently object in all probability. He had never got over her recklessness in throwing up a steady job to go into business on her own as a jewellery designer. Even now with the premises at the end of Provence Street nearly ready as a combined showroom and home for herself, he was reluctant to admit she had made a success of things. He'd be even less likely to admit she could afford an impulsive generous gesture to himself and Deidre. He'd probably tell her to stop swanking, remind her that chickens should be hatched before counting and that customers had not yet rolled up into the new premises.

In sudden impatience she closed her thought on the idea of making the offer. She said lightly, "I'm going to wash your hair and curl it into a pony tail ready for school in the morning. What possessed you to decide you'd like to try plaits?"

Ann's plump hands fingered the tight little pigtails. "Judy has them," she ventured rather plaintively.

"And you have to keep up with the Judys of the school set? Do you really yearn for plaits? Or shall it be a pony tail again?"

"Oh, a pony I expect. I think I'll draw a flame tree, but this book isn't nearly as good as the other you know. *This* has . . ."

"Shiny paper. I know, pet," Rachel pulled herself to her feet. "And I'll have a shiny nose if I sit on top of the fire. You can draw me under the flame tree, shiny nose and all, if you like."

.   .   .

He sat on the motor-scooter, so still he could have been welded in the materials that made the machine. The whole place was quiet and deserted. If anyone was home in the quiet street of Acacia Way there was no sign of it and the house he was watching, the sort of place Ivy called "worthy" because of its solid brick face, seemed sunk in introversion among the huddle of trees in front of it.

Now that he was there his brain seemed to have dulled into futility. He couldn't think what to do next—of how he was going to find if it was the right place. It took him a long time before he realised he had made the journey for nothing; that he should have picked up the phone again in the call-box and rung the number and asked to speak to Mrs. Swan. He'd heard her voice there by the lake. He didn't know if he would recognise it again, but he could say something to her—something . . . on the lines of what he had said to Miss Thatcher, of course. He could say, "I saw your little girl in the reserve, Mrs. Swan and there's a . . ." what? . . . "a parcel, a book, a

33   UN—C

pencil . . . I thought maybe it was hers." And the woman would say, wouldn't she, if she and the child had been there?

He kicked the scooter into life and went back to the call-box. The tobacco smell seemed stronger as though someone had been in there since himself and had stood there smoking while talking.

His fingers were cold and wet and fumbling with the coins and the dial, but finally he had dialled and this time the call was answered almost at once.

It was a man who answered.

That was a shock in itself. He'd been so hoping that the husband would be away and that the house would be empty except for the woman and the child, so that when the child was asleep, he could simply have walked up to the door.

"Hello, who's there?" the question came brusquely, speaking of a Sunday quiet interrupted; repulsing the thought of invasion of Sunday privacy.

He was suddenly frightened the receiver would be slammed down before he had said all he had to. He blurted out, "The little girl. Judith. Judith Swan. I want to talk to her . . ." then was furious because he had asked for the child and not the woman.

Then he thought that the mistake might be a good one. The woman might have started questioning. The child would simply say, "Yes I was there" or "No, I wasn't". Wouldn't she?

But the man was asking, "Who's this?"

"You wouldn't know me. It's the little girl . . ."

There was a sound curiously between a snort and a guffaw. "My kid's nine years old. Didn't think she was old enough for boy friends . . . hold on . . ."

He could still hear the bellowing voice. Fainter, but still there. It was saying, "Phone for Judy. Some man. Says we don't know him, but Judy does. What d'you make of that, Ag?"

There was a murmur, distant, then a rattle, and a sharp, high voice, suspiciously demanding, "Who's this? I'm Mrs. Swan. Who're you?"

It couldn't be her, he thought dazedly. He couldn't fit the shrill, high voice to the pale-faced slim woman by the lake. Her voice had been deep. He remembered that now. Deep for a woman. Not like this one at all.

"Who's there? Who is it? What do you want?" The questions came in suspicious rapid-fire that made him blurt out into speech while he was still trying to think what to do; to hold her talking; to make certain about her.

He blurted out, "Your little girl was in the reserve and I saw her and I want to talk to her. I want to . . ."

He could picture the red of indignation and rage, of panic, sweeping into the sort of face that went with a sharp, high voice like hers, as she broke in, "You just get off this line. You just ring this number again or try following my little girl around and . . ."

He cut her short in the middle of it. He knew she wasn't the woman he wanted. He started to snigger in long gasping breaths as he stood there. The idea that she imagined he was the type who followed little girls was somehow startlingly funny.

But then the laughter died. Now he knew Mrs. Swan wasn't the one he had to try to work out which house in Fielding Street held Mrs. English.

•   •   •

At half past five it was dark, water thudding on the roof, gurgling down piping, dripping on pathways under the trees. Rachel had gone out to drive her little car into the shelter of the side garage, watching and listening, seeing a few dim street lights, hearing only the gush and rustle of the storm. None of the houses she could see had lights at the front. It was as though the whole town had drawn into separate little cocoons of hibernation till the weather cleared.

35

Her run back was in tiptoe jumps across the gleaming puddles that reached between garage and house. Because the front door faced the south it took the full force of her two arms to push it closed behind her and her coming in tore a gust through the house, slamming doors inside, twitching a lace-edged runner from the hall table into a white-capped peak.

Straightening it, she went on into the sitting-room where Ann was crouched in front of the fire, her head bent and the fine light brown hair flopping forwards over her face while she brushed at it with long sweeps of a blue-backed brush.

There was a pleasant smell in the room compounded of scented shampoo, of drying hair, of hot mugs of cocoa and the smell of warmth from the fire. Rachel, going forward to take the brush, wielding it more vigorously than the child, remembered how once in their childhood Roger had heard her say something like that and had protested warmth didn't have a smell of its own. But it did, she reflected. In the centre of it, brought out by it, was the scent of polish from the furniture, the resin and tang in the red-leafed branches from a flame tree that Deidre had put on top of the piano and even the print smell of the books, warmed in their shelves. She sat savouring it, picking out each separate item of it as she brushed rhythmically and a teenage pop singer wailed sadly of love from the depths of the radio.

"You can't be enjoying that, Ann," she said at last. "If you go on listening to much more of the same you'll grow up with the idea that love and gall-stones are the same painful stomach-ache."

There was a muffled giggle under the flopping brown hair. Rachel parted the softness of it, holding it back either side of the fire-flushed round face. She said, "What say you invite someone over? I'll offer to act as chauffeur if necessary and we'll go collect whoever you choose. How about the pigtailed mopper you yearn to be like? Judy? Well?"

"She'd have to eat with us," Ann pointed out with devasta-

36

ting candour, "and there's only just a little bit of meringue pie left and I *like* meringue pie."

"Maybe Judy doesn't. She could be a prunes and custard girl."

"No, she's not. We could maybe eat first though, and then ring her and if she's fed she could come on over."

"My angel child! You take your chance on having a full guest or an empty one in this life and if it's the latter you hand over the meringue pie with a wide smile. If you prefer the pies of this world you just do without the friends, my treasure."

"That," Ann agreed, with sweet simplicity, "is just what daddy says — that you'll never marry because you can't bear a man to have a finger in the pie where your affairs are concerned."

. . .

It had taken several minutes for him to find a name against an address in Fielding Crescent and when he rang he collected only the monotonous engaged signal. Either J. D. Monaghue was gossiping or else he was slumbering peacefully and had taken the receiver off the hook to make sure he wouldn't be disturbed.

Rage flamed through him and the waste of time. He pressed the recall button viciously, collected the coins and started a second hunt through the directory. Finally his finger halted. His lips mouthed the number and one plump stubby finger dialled.

This time there was no engaged signal. Only a long wait and then a pleasant feminine voice repeating the number he had been mouthing.

At the sound of it he had jerked into attention, trying to place it against the voice heard in the reserve. It had taken him a couple of seconds of confusion before he remembered this woman couldn't be the one he was seeking.

She repeated the number, her voice holding a question mark at the continued silence.

His work-hour smoothness honeyed his tongue again. "Mrs.

Olwin? I'm truly sorry disturbing you this way. I want to apologise for that. You see, I'm looking for someone called English. Along your road. I had the address but I've mislaid the number. I didn't want to come right along the road knocking folk up on a Sunday, of all times, and I looked for a name in the directory that was in Fielding Street, and yours . . ."

"English?" The breaking-in wasn't impatient. She sounded pleased that she was able to help. "That's number four and it's right the other end of us. A red brick with green paint, though you won't be able to see that clearly in this downpour. But it's right the other end—the end by Ronald Street, if you know that?"

"Yes."

"But I happen to know Don English isn't home." The voice was regretful now. She didn't know how in the box he was tensing, exultant. "He's in the farm machinery line and . . . but I expect you know that. It'll be about business you want to see him, of course?"

"Yes," he answered again.

"Well, I happen to know he's not home. He was going north this week and the trip's too far back just for the weekend and he's staying over up there. I thought I'd mention it to save you a trip out and if there's some message I could send maybe send my boy over . . ."

"It doesn't matter. Not at all. No message." He was angry now and impatient at her solicitude, her pleasant-voiced effort to help. He wanted her to ring off so he could get moving again, so he could visit the house with the red brick and the green paint.

He rang off, the smoothness gone out of his voice and manner. If she thought anything of it she'd put it down to him being angry at not being able to see Don English. Wouldn't she? Then he spent five frantic minutes wondering what would happen when the woman . . . when Mrs. English . . . wasn't around any more to talk of whom she'd seen in the reserve. Would this Mrs. Olwin he'd rung remember the call and how she'd told a stranger Mrs. English was without a man in the house? Calming again he reassured himself it didn't matter, that it would be all to the good if she did remember and speak out. Because the police would put it down to a prowler making sure the house was free of a man; put it down to someone getting ready to go up to the house and lure the woman out.

So he didn't have to worry any more about it.

.   .   .

They'd reached a compromise. Ann would ring Judy and suggest she came over and bring anything she liked to add to what Rachel had described as "pot luck". They'd pool the result and Judy would have first choice of what there was, meringue pie included.

Rachel stayed in the sitting-room, reaching for cigarettes, one ear cocked to the sound of Ann dialling, to the sound of her small voice asking for Judy. With interest she noted that her fingers were slightly trembling as she held a match to the cigarette. She knew it was with temper.

Yet it was unreasonable to be angry. Completely unreasonable because she must have realised, quite often, without giving conscious light to the thought, that Roger and Deidre must have discussed her spinsterhood quite frequently and quite openly and debated the reasons for it. Unreasonable again, because she knew Roger considered her too bossy and too independent for her own good.

It was still a goad to her pride to have the knowledge shoved down her throat by Ann that her brother considered her too bossy and independent to be a marriageable prospect, to be attractive to any man.

She wondered what he and Deidre would say if she came out into the open and told them the truth—that she wanted to marry Stephen Linquist, and that he had no intention of bringing the pleasant dream to reality because her very femininity, her very desirability in his eyes, made her a dependency that he refused to afford.

Stephen had gained a unique position as news editor on the local radio station. His was the quiet controlled voice that was listened to every evening and every morning by people who had no conception of the hours in between; of the snatched sleep, of the countless interviews, of the constant travelling; of the prying and pressures that made up the half hour morning and evening when he spoke of all he had learned in the time between.

And now there was more ahead of him. She might never see him again. She'd had to face up to that, because from South America he might go to the opposite side of the world, or the Poles, or wherever there was news, and trouble. And no place for a woman.

Because there was danger and always would be wherever he went he considered there was no place in his life for her. She, being a woman, belonged where she was now, in a medium-sized country town. Safe and secure, with her own business, her own car, a good income, furniture she could polish and shine and know it was hers and not the fittings of some rented, temporary place to sleep and eat. It was useless to tell him she wanted neither furniture, nor settled home, security, or independence or safety. He had made the decision for her and because she was a woman and couldn't simply follow him willy-nilly, she was going to say goodbye and pretend with a smile to Roger and Deidre and all the rest of the world that her heart was still in one safe, secure, icy-cold piece.

She said, "What?" and came out of the painful abstraction of her thoughts to realise that Ann was waiting patiently for her to listen to something.

Satisfied that attention was gained at last Ann said rapidly, "Judy can't come. Her mother won't let her out. And she wants to talk to you. Mrs. Swan does. Not Judy."

"Ha! Your meringue pie is safe." Rachel ruffled the light

brown hair that still trailed, straight, nearly dry, loosely over the child's shoulders and back, and went to the phone, curling up in the blue chair by the little desk, with her long legs under her, as she said into the receiver, "Mrs. Swan? It's Rachel. Rachel Penghill. Ann's Aunt."

"Why yes, of course." The voice was rapid and shrill and anxious. "I know you, you know. We've met."

Rachel cast her thoughts into memory for recollection, gained nothing and merely said, "Oh?", but the elder woman wasn't asking for recollection. She was asking, Rachel realised, for reassurance in her panic.

"Miss Penghill, I'm quite upset. Ann wanted Judy to come on over, but I'm just not game to let her out. You see he rang up this way and he sounded so queer and I don't like it and my husband doesn't either. You read such awful things . . ."

"He? Who rang?"

There was a silent hesitation, a faint little husky breath of laughter that held no amusement. The voice was steadier when Mrs. Swan spoke again.

"I'm sorry. I'm so rattled I'm babbling, aren't I? But I don't like it. It was this way. A while back—oh, it must be twenty minutes or so now, a man rang. He asked to speak to Judy and my husband thought it funny, because it was a man. Not a boy. Not even a boy whose voice had broken. We could tell. It was a man and Judy's only nine and Fred, my husband you know, thought it was downright queer Judy having a man calling her.

"But when I went to see who it was he . . . well he said he'd seen Judy. In the reserve I think he said. And he wanted to talk to her. He sounded funny. Excited and tensed up, you know. I can't really explain, but I'm not imagining things. And it was the words he said, and the way he said it—well obviously he was one of *those*. And he knows Judy's name even and our address. He must have been following her around, mustn't he?

41

"When I got angry and started to tell him off he just rang off."

A scene jumped sharply into focus in Rachel's thoughts—herself and the falling leaves and the cold tingle of air on her face and the man—golden-haired, blank-faced, staring at her, mumbling at her and stumbling away.

She wondered, suddenly uneasy, if it had been Ann the man had been after. She remembered how he had stared at the child—so intently that her own gaze had turned anxiously, afraid that Ann was in some trouble—had fallen over or stumbled on a snake among the leaves. And then he had looked at herself. And gone away. Frightened away? From the child? Because there was an adult there?

She was suddenly furiously angry, with a cold sliver of panic down her spine, but she knew that she wasn't going to admit it. The woman on the phone was panic-stricken already. She wasn't going to add fuel to the panic with her own tale. That could be told to Roger. And to Deidre. In the morning. There was no hurry about it. Ann was quite safe, and so was Judy. So was every child, she thought thankfully. For tonight. There'd be no child out in the streets, in quiet spots, in this downpour. So there was no hurry to get hold of Roger and ask his advice about it.

And certainly no need to frighten Mrs. Swan further.

She said soothingly, "You must have had a shock, but it does happen you know—probably all he meant to do—I know it sounds ghastly—but he probably was going to talk a lot of filth to Judy. That's about all that type would do. If he rang up," the certainty was growing in her as she spoke that she was right, "it's a good bet he meant to do exactly that. If he was going to try and get hold of Judy he'd have waited till he found her alone somewhere—not rung up. Now wouldn't he?"

"Well, bless you!" There was a shaky laugh. "I never thought of that, you know. Neither did Fred. We've been questioning Judy and she can't remember any man staring at her or following her. I'll tell Fred what you say. I was all for ringing the police right off, but Fred said the man wasn't likely to be round here and after all it's Sunday. No need to go rushing to them. We could just report it tomorrow say. You've relieved my mind, though. I thought . . . well somehow I expected to look up and see him sticky-beaking through the windows or trying to get in . . ."

"Mr. Swan's right. He wouldn't hang round, in case you've rung the police, Mrs. Swan," Rachel's voice was a soothing drone now. "If I were you I'd just see that young Judy doesn't get to the phone first in the next few days."

"I'll do that. I'll see she doesn't get near it."

For a long moment Rachel went on sitting there. Her first impulse was to question Ann; ask her if she'd seen the golden-haired man anywhere. But Ann, she remembered, hadn't seen the man that day in the reserve. To start questioning her might only frighten her. It was up to Roger and Deidre to do something about it. Ann was safe for tonight. And so was everyone else.

For the first time she was glad of the downpour.

.   .   .

The house was dark at the front, like all the others in Fielding Street, except one, halfway down where a lantern light was glowing beside the front door. He left the scooter in the shadows round the corner and came back, soft-footed on the wet sidewalk. He didn't open the gate. If the hinge screeched it could be heard even over the noise of the storm and someone could come out. He didn't want that—until he was out of sight.

There was only a low stone fence at the front. He vaulted it easily and went round the side of the house. He could see lights then, in the wide window that was partly shielded by venetians. He could see someone—a woman—moving round behind the slats of it, but he couldn't see what she looked like. She was just a feminine shape. Nothing more.

And he had to see her, to make absolutely certain he was at the right place. And when he was certain he was going to have to wait. Till late. When the child was sent off to bed and he could knock the woman up on some excuse and get into the place or get her outside.

But first he had to see her.

He wasn't conscious of the water on his face; of the slow soddenness seeping into his jeans. He was only conscious of the half brick in his right hand, and what he was doing.

The brick fell with a resounding crash against the side of the house. It made more noise than he expected and he saw the shadow behind the blind become still. Then it moved and a little later the door he was watching flew open.

The woman was peering out and the child was with her, too. He could hear them discussing what had happened. He wasn't worried about that. They'd put it down to something to do with the storm.

He wanted only to see them and when he did—when the woman actually stepped out into the rain, shielding her head with what looked like a tea-towel—a gay printed thing—he nearly cried out in sheer rage.

Because it wasn't her. And in a minute he knew it wasn't the child either. Both of them were strangers.

CHAPTER FOUR

"My daughter's a good girl. There's never been any trouble, never a word said against her and you can ask anyone and get. the same answer . . ." the repetitive, anxious voice followed them down the cream-painted hall, along the grey and black check linoleum, into the bedroom with the pictures of pop stars on the walls and a huge teddy bear stuck on top of the mirror-fronted wardrobe.

Sergeant Giddings didn't listen. He had heard it before. The anxious frightened words of relatives who were facing the police for the first time, having to admit that a member of the family had done something that could have raised eyebrows, were something he knew well.

Because her actions could have raised eyebrows sky high, couldn't they, he was pondering tiredly as he looked down at the girl in the narrow bed. She looked childish with her black hair spread out on the white pillow and her face pale and blotched with tears, but he guessed how she'd looked earlier that day—primped to the nines, he thought. And asking for trouble.

"Never a word . . ." the anxiety behind him was a thing of sheer pain and terror.

He turned, his square, suntanned face kind, his grey eyes a little tired. He was looking at a woman much of his own half century in years, much of a greyness of hair, but sparse and work-tired, fragile-looking against his own uniformed bulk.

He said gently, "Now don't you worry, Mrs. Gault. Don't you worry."

"Never a word . . ."

"I know. It's just the way, isn't it? Lightning hits when and

45

where you'd never expect." Thirty years of dealing with other people's sorrows and failures and petty and grievous sins had made him adept at soothing clichés. He could see the gratitude in the pale eyes and under it the shame because there was a policeman in the house—something to be explained tomorrow and all the tomorrows afterwards to the neighbours and anyone curious enough to read in the papers what the girl had been up to.

Because she'd be in them. His gaze switched to the pale narrow face and his expression hardened. The girl would enjoy it. As soon as the fright was over she would enjoy the sensation, even the trial. There'd be a vindictive pleasure in her at the man getting caught and being put behind bars. There'd be no shame in her, or even real knowledge of the fact that she had asked for trouble.

He said to the woman, "How about making a cup of tea all round, Mrs. Gault, while I talk to Rose?" He made it sound as though the talk would be an easy thing; as though there was no need at all for her to stay and keep watch and protect the girl. After a moment she nodded, essayed a vague smile at him and went out, leaving him there in a straight-backed chair by the bed, with the constable, young, stolid, blank-faced, standing in the doorway.

Giddings cleared his throat again. His gaze was steady on the narrow pale face as he demanded, "What were you wearing today, Miss Gault?"

She hadn't expected that and her lips parted in surprise. He could see the small white sharp teeth, one of them at at the front crossing slightly over its neighbour.

"I . . . everything I had on's ruined." Her fingers were plucking at the top sheet. "My skirt and twinset . . ."

"Your good things? You were dressed up?"

"Well, yes," her eyes were round and blank and surprised still.

"You had a date with this chap then? A date settled and

46

made days ago? Yesterday? Early this morning?" He pressed at each continued shake of her dark head.

"No date then? So why'd you dress up?"

He had her on the defensive. He didn't feel any compunction at keeping her there. "You left home with the idea of getting a date? Of picking some man up?"

Her voice was shrilly defensive, "What's the harm in thinking you could maybe run into friends? In wanting t'look . . ."

"No harm. So this chap's a friend? You know him well? What's his name?"

"Mart."

"Mart who?"

"Dunno."

Her eyes were hating him because she had expected sympathy. In a minute she'd try tears, he thought without compassion.

"Just Mart. Funny you don't know his other name when you're friends, isn't it?"

"All right, come off it and quit jeering at me." The young voice cracked high in anger and defiance. "He's not a friend, but he looked all right and besides I've seen him round'n . . ."

"Where'd you pick him up?"

"Just . . . in the street. I was waiting for a bus . . ."

The constable coughed. The sound was loud and explosive. Giddings didn't look up. He went on gazing at the narrow white face. His voice changed suddenly and was nearer to the tone he had used to the woman, "What happened?"

She told him jerkily, her voice getting huskier and huskier, one hand pressed to her bruised throat before she had finished. There'd been talk—about what he was going to do—cars he was going to buy. Silly talk. She'd known he wasn't in the class that could buy that sort of thing; live the sort of life he was chattering about. She'd told him to lay off; that he was a fool and ought to be locked up. He'd started in shaking her and she'd been mad. Yes, she'd hit out at him, she admitted

47

huskily. And he'd grabbed her by the throat. At first she'd been just plain wild. She'd been thinking of what she would say and do when she got free. Only she hadn't been able to. She thought she had actually fainted for a bit. She had been conscious again of him shaking her over and over and she'd had the sense to play dumb. She was frightened of what he'd do; that he might try to silence her completely for fear she'd tell the police on him.

And after a while he'd stopped shaking her. She'd played possum and held her breath till she had nearly burst, she told Giddings tearfully. Then, unbelievably, he'd started dragging her along and next thing she had found herself in the lake. She had still tried to pretend she was right out, but finally she had had to give up, turn over, come up for air. And he'd been gone. She'd managed to drag herself on to the side of the grass again but she hadn't been able to walk. Even when the rain had started she'd just had to lie there.

Then she had been ill. Finally she had managed to get out of the reserve and get to one of the farms. They'd put her in a car and brought her home and mum had got the doctor and then the police.

She didn't want to get anyone into trouble. Her voice had settled into a whine. Giddings' face was impassive as he went on listening to it. She'd only rung the police . . . and she'd never ever been in trouble and he could ask mum or anyone, if he didn't believe her . . . but she didn't think he, Mart, was safe. The funny way he'd talked and the way he'd glared at her and . . . he just wasn't safe. And she was scared blue.

"A pity she *isn't* blue. Black and blue. Where she sits down," Giddings commented as he slid into the police car with the constable getting in behind the wheel. "Now about this Mart . . ." he was reflecting on the girl's last statement, her shrill, protesting defensive:

"But I wouldn't've gone with him only I knew him. That's

48

straight. I've seen him round. He works in Spencers. The men's wear in Provence Street."

"I know him . . . *of* him, sir," the constable corrected himself quickly. His pleasant face was still blank, as though he was fearful of showing the wrong expression. He reminded Giddings of himself, thirty years before, when he'd been scared . . . scared blue as Rose Gault might say . . . of putting a foot wrong.

"Well?" he encouraged, "if you know him it'll save us a lot of time."

"Martin Deeford, sir. That's his full name. Can't remember the address but it'll be in records." At the sharp look from the other he shook his head. "Not what you're thinking, sir. No trouble that way. He runs a scooter. There was a minor set-to about three months back. Deeford was in the right. The car driver in the wrong."

"What's he like?"

"Smooth-mannered, affable . . ." the constable seemed to have run dry of adjectives.

"Did he fly off the handle over the accident the way he did with the girl?"

"No sir. Smug. That was him. He was in the right, conscious of it and very affable. An upright, clear-of-conscience citizen helping the police." He grinned suddenly.

"Using three words where one would do . . . yes, I know what you mean. All right, we'll get his address and call. If he's home it'll be easy. If he's out . . . as I impressed on the Gault woman, it's a case of keeping quiet. He must think he did the girl in and he's either run for it or he thinks he's safe. If the former we'll have a lot of hard work, and if the latter he'll come home sometime—if he doesn't find out the girl's still alive. If he does, he'll run, so it's important they keep quiet for the next few hours. He wouldn't have rolled her into the lake, I'm certain, unless he thought she was dead. If he imagined she was still able to put him in for what had happened he'd

UN—D

have tried smoothing her down, not adding to the mess by tossing her into the water.

"We'll have to see if there wasn't someone else out there—someone who saw the pair of them. A good lawyer'd make mincemeat of the girl. I remember one case a good few years back where the same sort of caper happened—a pick-up and assault. The girl swore herself blind it was some chap she knew vaguely from seeing him around. It wasn't. But it turned out they were fairly alike and she'd made an honest enough mistake at first and the chap had kidded her along. She must have known differently of course, when she saw the chap she'd named in a line-up, but by then she was thinking what her family'd say and everyone else, too. She'd embroidered the story by then—made it seem she'd spoken to the chap several times. Made out it wasn't just a pick-up. She wouldn't give in, but fortunately the man she'd named had been somewhere else. That was all saved his skin.

"You'll see, this Deeford's lawyer will make out it's the same sort of case. If she's picked up men before there'll be girl friends who'll know and who'll talk. If we can find someone else who saw them together it'll give us a decent chance to put him away for a bit. We'll have to put a call out for anyone who was by the lake, but not now. Not till we have him pinned. The main thing now is not to frighten him into running."

"He might confess to the lot and save any trouble at all," the constable ventured hopefully.

Giddings' mouth went down in derision. "Think any lawyer would let that stick? He'd recant it in court with a charge of police brutality, plus the lawyer claiming the girl'd named the first chap she thought of to save herself getting called a cheap little tart. She had to give some story to her mum—she couldn't just laugh off those bruises. No, I want another witness. Someone who saw them together. But that'll wait. We'll get his address and see if he's home . . ."

•   •   •

When he suddenly thought of Rose it was like thinking of something remote that hardly touched him. His mind was filled with only one thought—the woman who had seen him and whose speaking out could put him in prison. His rage against her was growing with the hours. She was a menace, a disaster that was threatening to engulf him in darkness he could never escape.

It was added fury to his panic that he had so far, with the hours speeding relentlessly by, failed to find her.

He stood there in the downpour long after the back door of the house had closed and the woman's shadow was passing back and forth behind the partly closed venetians again, groping painfully at inspiration to tell him what to do next. He had thought first of ringing Miss Thatcher again. Then he hadn't dared. She would only wonder why he was insistent, so desperate, to find the child, when it was a simple matter of a parcel left behind; a matter she had promised to fix herself in the morning.

He had thought of, and discarded, ringing Judith Swan again and asking her—describing the child in the park and asking her who it was. But he had known that wouldn't work. Most likely the parents would answer, his previous call still sharp in their thoughts and they'd likely slam down the receiver and summon the police. Not that that worried him. He wouldn't be around to be picked up. But it wasn't going to help him. And if he got the child . . . by now she'd have been questioned over and over by the mother. If he started in questioning her about another child she'd tell her parents for a certainty. Even if she gave him the other one's name, she'd still tell. The mother by now would be seeing shadows where none existed. She'd jump straight to the conclusion another child was in danger and make a phone-call or a journey—either way put the woman on her guard.

He didn't know the names of any of the other school-teachers, of any of the children. He didn't know . . .

Then he thought of the child dancing among the fallen leaves of the flame trees. Had there been a practised air to her movements? He simply didn't know. But he was remembering the thud-thud-thud that filled his Saturday mornings. Three doors away, in the upstairs room over the greengrocer's, but it could still be heard in Spencers' shop where he stood behind the counter with a fixed, pleasant smile and affable manner. When he'd first been at Spencers the sound had puzzled him till old Spencer had told him it was the little girls' dancing class run by Mrs. Spinks.

So if the child went to dancing class Mrs. Spinks would know her, wouldn't she?

．　　　．　　　．

Rachel had come to the conclusion that the Sunday evening children's show on TV was a mixed blessing. On the one hand it kept Ann occupied and quiet; on the other it ruled out the use of the radio because, as Ann had pointed out at the first clouding of the screen, the use of one ruled out the other for some odd reason and had been doing so for days and her mother kept forgetting to call the mechanic to see what was wrong.

That left Rachel herself to watching the antics of what she privately thought was a pair of morons, or simply thinking. Thinking was disastrous because her thoughts turned straight to Stephen. It was neither productive nor comforting or even sensible and she tried switching to something else. The something else wasn't comforting either, producing only vague fears which she tried washing out of her mind with a deluge of common-sense, reminding herself that the house was safe and so was Ann and that a worrying call and an intense stare in a quiet park could be turned into very little or a lot, depending on whether you used common-sense or panic.

She wished though that she had never seen the man in the reserve; never seen the light through the flame trees shine on his golden hair, or watch his strange dazed expression as he looked at her. He had looked . . . what? . . . odd. The more she thought about it the more she knew she disliked the remembrance of his intense look at Ann's dancing figure and the dazed blankness of the round face turned to herself.

It was stomach-churning to think that one day soon Ann could lift the receiver and hear a low rapid voice spilling out the filth of a perverted mind. Useless to try the consoling thought that a nine-year-old would be unlikely to understand a hundredth part of it. It would still be horrible. And part of it, understood or not, would stick in her mind, to fester there, to be whispered over, probably, with other children, till she discovered some garbled idea of what it really meant.

Then relief came to the pressure of unpleasant conjecture. The matter was simply solved. She had told Mrs. Swan what to do. Roger and Deidre, once they knew, would simply see that Ann never answered the phone.

Then uneasiness, panic, shot back in the blinding question — what if he comes to the door? Sees Ann alone? Or follows her in the street and corners her? Spilling filth at her through half smiling mouth.

It was a useless exercise in sheer panic, she told herself in sudden fury. Useless to think about it. Useless to worry too. It was up to Roger and Deidre to see that none of the unpleasant possibilities came to be a fact. Ann was safe enough for that evening.

I'll speak to Sandy before I go, she promised herself. Warn her not to let Ann near the phone; not to answer the door without knowing who is there. And tomorrow . . . she'd see Roger. Before he left for work. In the morning. Everything would be all right and quite safe until then.

CHAPTER FIVE

To Ivy Deeford police on the doorstep meant trouble. She wondered if it showed in her face as she stood there in the hall, clasping her cardigan around her plump figure, against the chill from the outside world. There'd been police on her doorstep other times. She tried to choke down the memory, the constriction in her throat, that came welling up every time she looked at a police uniform.

But she couldn't control the sharp question, the anxiety that jumped to her tongue and spilled out in a hurried, "What's happened?"

So it was like that, Giddings thought tiredly, looking into the features that were carefully controlled into blankness in spite of her betraying tongue. He'd heard that same question plenty of times, always from people who had something to hide or some memory of past trouble that they wanted to forget. Then, before he could grasp at the words and ask why she suspected, just at the bare sight of him, that something was wrong, she had corrected herself, trying to retrieve her mistake with a quick, "I'm always on the jump while my brother's out on that blessed scooter. They're such bits of things and when you see some of these big trucks roaring along . . . it's the dread of my life I'll open the door and there'll be a policeman on the step to say there's been some dreadful mishap and . . ."

"Your brother had an accident about three months back, didn't he?" he cut her short.

He saw the relief slide into her blue eyes. Her big flabby body seemed to shrink fully a couple of inches down onto itself from the upright rigidity of fear and panic that had been holding her. She said, puzzlement and relief both in her placid

54

voice, "I thought that was all over and done with. 'Twasn't Mart's fault in the first place." Then anxiety came back. She asked sharply, "You mean you're here to say there's been another crash? Is he hurt? Bad?"

"No. We'd better come in, Miss Deeford."

She didn't protest. She led the way into a small room at the front, switching on the light and a small electric fire, gesturing them to the dark leather settee against the wall.

"What is it?" she demanded.

"I'd like to see your brother."

"He isn't in."

"What time will he be back, do you know?"

"I don't."

She sat, feet solidly flat on the floor, her knees a little splayed under the olive green wool of her dress, stolidly staring at him, waiting patiently.

"Has he been out all day?"

For the first time she hesitated, turning over the question as though she suspected there was danger in it. At last she said, "No. He went out and came in and went out again."

He finally got from her the fact that the man had gone straight out after lunch at mid-day. He hadn't offered to wash up. The fact rankled with her under her wariness and anxiety. He had pleaded meeting a friend and being late. He'd come back about half past four, changed and gone out again.

"He was wet through," she volunteered, choosing each word with care. The slowness of her speech betrayed that. "I wanted him to stay on in but he said he was invited out somewhere."

"Did he say where? Did he take some things with him? A suitcase maybe?"

She stared in astonishment, "Why'd he want a suitcase to go out for? I would've asked what he thought he was playing at, wouldn't I've? No, he just slipped on a slicker over dry things. He hadn't taken the slicker before, though I told him noontime it was going to come on this way, but you can't give Mart advice.

55

He just gets stubborn. He was sodden when he came on back."

"Where'd he been? Did he say?"

"Shooting." Her lips compressed.

"What time will he be back?"

"He didn't say."

"Did he say not to get a meal for him tonight?"

The frizz of butter-yellow hair jerked as she shook her head. "No need. He knows it's cold cuts, get them yourself, Sunday evening. Always is." Then her anxiety exploded into a frantic, defiant, "But I've no call to be sitting here answering you this way. What do you want with Mart? What's it to you what he's up to?"

He told her.

Used as he was to the many ways, most of them bitter, that his disclosures were taken, there was still compassion in him for the way hope drained out of her eyes and body, but he noted grimly that there was no protest, no denial that the man could have acted so.

When she continued sitting stolid, silent, he suggested, "There's been trouble before, hasn't there?"

"Considering you'd soon ferret it all out there's no use me saying anything else."

"He has a record, has he?"

"Yes. He was put in when he was sixteen. Three years back. He got in a rage and strangled a dog. In front of some kids. He always had a temper. There'd been . . . there'd been trouble before. Things I hushed up. I thought when he got bigger . . . anyway he was running wild then. They said he needed a man to handle him so he was put in a home. And there was more trouble. Mart said it wasn't all his fault. Maybe so. I wasn't around to know. He said one of the men in the place kept picking on him. Maybe so. Mart lost his temper and half choked him. He's strong you see. Got a right hand like a vice. His left arm's not much good. Hasn't been since an accident when he was a mite. He can't lift it much. He's got a good grip

56

with the hand though and he's exercised, made his right one make up for it. And when he gets hold . . . anyway they let him out finally. And we moved house."

"Here?"

"Not at first. We came twelve months back. First there was another place. Mart couldn't settle, and there was trouble. Mart went for his boss that time. I got it hushed up." Her voice was suddenly bitter. "It didn't come to me till later on that the business was a bit shady and the boss didn't want your sort around any more than I did. So it got hushed up. And we moved and changed our name."

"What was it?" he asked sharply.

"Ford. My middle initial is D. I added it. Deeford, see. I held the old trouble over his head here. Any more violence I told him and any more running around with a mob that's no good and I hand you straight in to the police and with the past at the back of you it'll go hard. So he behaved. Went to work in Spencers tame as a mouse. Never a scrap of trouble . . ."

He said bluntly, "The girl said he talked a lot of rubbish and got violent when she told him he was crazy, and that he ought to be locked up."

She nodded. "He's always been that way. A dreamer, with big ideas. Trouble is his dreams and fact all get mixed up together sometimes and he can't tell one from another, and he gets wild if someone doubts . . . and her saying that, reminding him . . . he can't bear the idea of being locked up again, Mart can't."

． ． ．

Mrs. Spinks was different from the others he had called. There was no sleep or resentment in her voice and she answered at once with a brisk, "May Spinks here."

He said smoothly, "I'm sorry for troubling you, Mrs. Spinks."

"You're not troubling me. I'm right here all alone." She made it sound like an invitation, as though she was hoping for a friendly contact to reach out and save her from herself. He wondered if her body was slumping in disappointment and petulance when he said, in that same smooth voice, "I'm going to ask a favour of your time, Mrs. Spinks. It's this way — I'm looking for a little girl who left a parcel in my shop. I know she was one of your little dancing girls and I thought . . . Mrs. Spinks would know. She's," his voice drowned her brief attempt to interrupt, "about nine I should think. A bit on the plump side with two brown pigtails. Would you know from that who she is, Mrs. Spinks?"

"No."

He could feel a pressure of fury building up in a tight band across his forehead. His tongue was tight clamped to the roof of his mouth to stop himself raging at her stupidity, in her refusal to help.

Then through the thickening cloud of anger he realised she was going on, "They don't have pigtails when they come to dancing class. If they've long hair — pony tails or braids or whatever, they let them loose for dancing and wear an Alice band or tie them up like a real ballerina."

"But you know who has long hair, who . . . ?" he began thickly.

"Of course I do. They're a constant irritation — the pins come out of the little buns and the ones with the band get floppier and floppier — they all finish up like a lot of shaggy ponies. So irritating and it spoils the look of the line. If you mean what you say about brown hair though, and the child being about nine, and plump, I'd say Ann Penghill or Judith Swan . . ."

"No," he said sharply.

"No?"

"Not the last, I mean. I . . . I know her."

"Then it would be Ann. Or else you're out in your age group. The others with long brown hair are all out of that age . . . above or below."

He said "Thank you" and put the phone down before she could ask the inevitable question as to the person speaking; before she could pry and get curious as to why her curiosity wasn't satisfied.

.   .   .

Ann had protested at an early bath, and had been overruled by Rachel's reasonable, "You're not going anywhere or having visitors so you can easily sit around in your pyjamas and dressing-gown. If you stay on top of the fire till bedtime the bathroom's going to feel like charity hall and I know the result . . . you'll dip one toe in the water and run for your life, my angel. And I shan't be here to see that you really scrub off the day's dirt."

She nearly added, "And scrub away the way that man's gaze rested on you," and uneasiness came back.

"Sandy will be here," Ann pointed out hopefully, to be met with the retort that it was doubtful if seventeen-year-old Alexandra Micklin would know a germ if she saw one and she certainly couldn't be expected to examine her charge's neck ears and back molars for signs of one.

"Daddy says," Ann contributed, "that the only thing Sandy would recognise at first sight is a boy, and that she's equipped with radar that goes beep-beep whenever one comes within a hundred feet."

"I doubt if you'd better repeat that to Sandy," Rachel told her dryly. "I doubt if she'd be flattered." Any more, she told herself grimly, than I was flattered on learning Roger's comments on myself.

Shooing her niece bathwards she asked suddenly, "Do you know any of Sandy's boy friends?"

"Oooh yes. There's Bryan who works in the bank but she doesn't like him any more and it's Lloyd mostly now. He's silly and calls me kiddo if I answer the phone when he rings if Sandy's here and . . ."

"Ann," Rachel knew that the sharpness of her voice was

59

surprising the child. She couldn't help it. She said curtly, "While Sandy's here tonight you're not to answer the phone. Understand? I've a special reason for asking. I want you to say it's all right. Well?"

"I'm not to answer the phone while Sandy's here," Ann parroted, her round blue eyes huge with curiosity.

"All right. Your parents will explain tomorrow probably. For tonight just remember your promise. Do you know," she was thinking again of the sudden idea that had come to her—that Sandy Micklin might know the golden-haired man—that she might be able to name him and say he was all right; disperse the vague unreasoning fears that kept returning to Rachel every time she thought of his intense stare at Ann and his vacant, dazed look at herself, "Do you know if one of Sandy's boys has golden hair? Really yellow hair?"

Ann bubbled through a mouthful of toothpaste suds and water, "She doesn't like'm with dyed 'air."

"I shouldn't think it was dyed," Rachel said reflectively.

Ann rinsed her mouth loudly and vigorously before demanding, "Who are you talking about?"

"Oh . . . just someone. Someone I saw. Don't worry your noodle over it and . . . there's the bell and Sandy, I expect. Hop into the tub and scrub . . . really scrub."

She thought in amusement that Sandy looked more impossible than ever as the girl minced into the hall on the pin-thin high black heels. She looked pathetically thin, too, with her uncurved body made skinnier and flatter by the tight mauve skirt and tightly belted leather car-coat. Even her hair, glossy brown, was tightened and thinned to the bones of her narrow head in a tight hard chignon that did nothing for her small face where the eyes showed enormous and somehow startled-looking in their maze of black liner and blue eyeshadow.

Sandy closed the huge black umbrella she had used for shelter and said breathlessly, "I got a lift over. Isn't it a stinker of a day, Miss Penghill?" Then she asked, rather uneasily, "Are you going to stay on?"

Rachel smiled wryly. She knew what Sandy intended the evening to be like. An early bed for Ann and then herself draped over the phone, talking to her boy friends with the intensity of seventeen years old. She didn't want an adult hanging around to curb her plans.

Rachel said briskly. "No. I promised to stay till you came. I'll be off as soon as Ann's out of the bath. You can leave her by the fire till bedtime."

"O.K." Sandy was pulling off the car-coat to reveal a mauve silk blouse under a beige cardigan.

"She can have milk if she wants to before she goes off, but don't fall for any please-please nonsense about cake and biscuit, will you? There's cold chicken in the frig' for you. Make a sandwich and there's cola, or make yourself a hot drink."

"O.K. Ta."

"And Sandy . . . this is important." Rachel hesitated, then went on, "Don't let Ann answer the phone. I've made her promise not to, but she might forget. There's been a bit of unpleasantness at another house. The little girl there—Judy Swan—was rung up by some man. Someone who'd seen her and followed her home, according to the mother. Mind you, there could be nothing in it except a bit of panic, but still . . . well it does sound like the type of thing that . . ."

"Oh, I know," Sandy nodded with an air of acute wiseness that would have been funny if Rachel hadn't been thinking again of the golden-haired man's intense stare at Ann. "The sort my mum says needs a good dose of Enos to get the badness out of them. If he tries it on here I'll give him salts enough to sting him good'n . . ."

"No, don't!" Rachel shook her head almost violently. "You couldn't handle that type, Sandy. It might only make him worse—even make him come to the door if he realised that

61

Ann was here alone with someone your age. If anything out of the way happens put down the phone and then ring the police . . . but honestly," the impatience in her voice was as much to reassure herself as Sandy, "it's probably nothing but a scare, blown up out of proportion."

Sandy said in a rush, "If you're worried, Miss Penghill, I could ring my Lloyd and ask him to come sit with me."

Rachel's uneasiness was lost in swift amusement, in a dry, "No you won't, Sandy. I know it would be glorious fun to have Lloyd to hold your hand all evening, but you know the rules here—no boys while you're sitting in this house."

Sandy's answering grin was sheepish, though she protested, "Honest, Miss Penghill, Lloyd and me're . . ."

"No go, Sandy. Rules are rules. Squint-eyed chinamen, escaped tigers, rogue elephants and boys come under the same heading while you're sitting with Ann. They don't cross the threshold or else . . ." she put finger to throat. "I'll leave the police number under the number where Mr. and Mrs. Penghill are. O.K.?"

"Roger!" Sandy grinned agreement.

"And Sandy . . ." Rachel turned back from the phone and the red-covered pad that Deidre kept there for messages, "talking of boys, do you know one round town who has golden hair? Really golden looking hair and . . ."

Sandy's nose wrinkled. "I don't go for that lot, Miss Penghill. I know it's all the rage for them to go blond, but they look silly. Honest."

"I don't think this one has dyed hair, Sandy, though of course I couldn't be sure."

She saw the open curiosity in the thin young face and smiled the question aside, "Not that it matters a jot. It was just someone I saw that I haven't seen before."

.   .   .

There was only one Penghill—R. Penghill and an address on Acacia Way. The fury came back when he saw that—when he

62

saw the number could be only a block at most from the Swan house. Then the fury went when he reflected that after all it hadn't mattered. He still had to wait till the child was in bed; till he could get the woman alone.

But first he had to make certain that he had really found her, the right one, at last. He stood there in the tobacco-scented mustiness of the box, sweating under the oilskin, wondering what to do this time.

He decided at last that he'd ring. That he'd ask for the woman and spin the same tale he had given to Mrs. Spinks and the school-teacher. He'd tell her a child had left a parcel in his shop . . . that day. He'd say that and she'd question the child. Wouldn't she? Then she might say something . . . even before questioning the child . . . along the lines of, "No, it couldn't have been Ann. We weren't shopping today. We were out by the lake." If she said that he'd know.

Even if she didn't he might recognise the voice that answered him. He tried, standing there, to remember the cadences of it, picturing her under the trees, but the voice was lost in a haze of memory; almost as lost as the thought of Rose and what had happened to her. Rose had become a secondary thing now; all he could think of was that woman was dangerous to him.

He hardly thought now of his first plan of seeing her alone and seeing if recognition and remembrance dawned in her pale face. That had become whirled down into the whirlpool of conviction that she knew him—that sometime in the past she had walked into Spencers and seen him; that she knew even his name; that soon she was going to say that name to the police.

The coins he put into the slot were the last from Ivy's rice caddy. He slid them in carefully, his fingers cold and clumsy, afraid that he would drop one and not find it again and that the rage of frustration would bring back the throbbing pain behind his eyes.

It was answered at once, with a single word, "Yes?" that gave him no clue at all.

He said, his thoughts suddenly blank, "Hello?"

And she said, as she'd said to him there by the lake, "Why, hello to you, too."

CHAPTER SIX

BECAUSE country towns didn't run to the number of police that would have made for really efficient running; because the small force had been depleted by one man off sick; because it was Sunday and because it was pouring, Giddings went out himself to the lake. The place had to be looked at sometime, and because there might be traces of the Deeford man left behind that would strengthen the police case in court, but the night's sodden downpour might disperse forever, the job couldn't be put off.

Rose had given a good description of where it had all happened, but even with that it was difficult to find the place in the downpour and darkness; worse to try and make some sort of search. Her purse, black suede with a gilt clasp, was there, the black colour coming off against the constable's fingers as he tried to brush off the clinging red leaves.

The constable said, "She won't thank us for giving it back like this."

"She won't thank us for anything." Giddings was cold and tired and irritable and didn't bother to hide it. He could feel the wet striking through the bottoms of his trouser legs, his hands and face were dripping and the cold from all three points seemed to be seeping right through his body. He said harshly, "If it wasn't for the fact Deeford sounds dangerous and lord knows what he might do in the future if he thinks he can get away with this job, I'd feel like thumbing my nose at it. I know that's a shock to your high ideals, son," he suddenly grinned into the wet face of the other man, "but I'm human, not a walking rule book that says every version of every crime is the same blasted thing.

"Know what'll happen when this blows over? Rose'll be back on the street corners ogling dates and picking up anyone in dance halls with a decent car, and if she gets into more trouble it'll be us to blame and not her, because we've failed to keep the town safe. So she and her mum and her Aunt Aggie and her second-cousin Susie and all the rest of the silly fools like her'll say. Find anything else?"

"Leaves, sir."

Giddings met the hint of sarcasm with a gentle, "Good. You go and find some more. You just take a walk right round the lake, keeping your lantern moving as far in as you can and see if there's traces of anyone else picnicking. The girl said it came on to rain all at once, didn't she? If there was anyone here—and ten to one we're out of luck and there wasn't a soul—they might have made a dash for it and left something behind. We can't afford to pass the point up. If anyone was around they might think twice about coming forward on our come-into-the-parlour pleas. Folk don't like getting involved in this sort of caper. If there was someone and we can get a lead to them . . . oh well, we've got to try. I want a water-tight case when we go to court."

They parted where Rose had rolled down into the lake, meeting again on the further bank. From there it was impossible to see, across the darkness, through the driving rain, where Rose and Martin Deeford had fought.

The constable's wet hands were held out mutely and Giddings gave a satisfied sigh as his own closed on the brown-paper-covered book.

"A kid's drawing-book." He delicately eased the wet pages away from each other. "And picnic scraps. That apple core hasn't been around longer than today, or the banana skin either. They ran for it all right, when the rain came. That means they were around when Deeford and the girl were here. Doesn't mean the pair were seen, but there's nothing to stop me hoping. So long as they saw Deeford come into the reserve

66

and can pick him out in a line-up we'll be jake. And if whoever it is doesn't fancy coming forward there's always the book. Easy enough to trace it."

"Just take it to school and let the kids say who owns it," the constable put in smartly.

Giddings grinned, trying to mop his wet face with an almost equally damp handkerchief. "Good man. That's just the idea. But it'll keep till the morning. I want Deeford charged and locked up before the news gets out. Tomorrow will do for witness-hunting."

.   .   .

Rachel said, "I was cut off," and stared at the receiver in blank surprise, then suddenly uneasiness came back. She wondered, replacing the receiver, not looking towards Sandy, whether it was the man who had spoken to the Swans—whether he had simply cut off when he realised it was a woman speaking and not a child.

I'm getting morbid, she thought in self-disgust—a real old woman with the mollycoddles. It was partly the weather, she told herself consolingly. No-one could listen to the downpour outside and not feel the misery of it soaking into every bone.

She said shortly. "Go on into the fire, Sandy. I'll get Ann out of the bath and into her pyjamas and then I'll be off."

"Have you got a date, Miss Penghill?" Sandy was examining her thin face in the hall mirror, a sudden look of anxiety in the thrust of her chin as she poked delicately at a small raised spot.

"No. I'm going to wash my hair, set it, put on a face mask and generally refurbish my middle-aged charms for the coming week's strife and toil."

Sandy giggled. "My Mum says middle-age is a state of mind and gets you any old time. She says she's been middle-aged since she was twenty-four and tried feeding and keeping four kids and herself and dad on what dad brings in. And you've never had to do that." She added with sudden grim determination in her young voice, "And I'm not going to do it

67

either. Mum doesn't like Lloyd but he gets good money in the garage and we've got it all settled. We're getting engaged next year and married the one after. We ought to have the down-pay on a house by then."

There was suddenly such wild envy in Rachel's body that it was sheer pain. She wanted to prick the bubble of Sandy's confidence; to say bitterly, "Things might go wrong, Sandy." She had to bring her teeth down hard on her bottom lip to stop the words springing out to life.

Then the phone rang again. She lifted the receiver, but didn't speak and a voice said "Hello".

She said, as she'd done before, her voice thick and strange to her own ears, "Why, hello to you, too," and heard laughter — Stephen's laughter.

"You always say that," his tone was light, mocking. "I've settled into the habit of saying simply 'hello' just to hear you say, 'Why, hello to you, too'."

Answering laughter warmed her voice when she said, "It's a bad habit. It doesn't sound business-like. I keep trying to break it," while her faint uneasiness at the last call slid away and was lost in the thought that it had been Stephen ringing and they had simply been cut off.

He said quickly, "I tried the shop first. Then I thought you might be over there and chanced . . ."

"I'm leaving now. In five minutes or so."

"Does that mean you've an appointment?"

She wondered what he would say if she said yes, if she invented some other man. Then she had the unpleasant feeling that he would probably be glad, because then he wouldn't have her unhappiness on his conscience; wouldn't reproach himself for letting her learn to love him when he had no intention of marrying her.

She said lightly, "With the coffee-pot, a bottle of shampoo and a face pack. There, now you know the dark secrets of my life."

She heard his chuckle. "Can I share the coffee-pot? The town's dead tonight."

She couldn't fight down the bitterness that burst out in the quick retort, "So you'll spare me fifteen minutes because you've nothing better to do?"

She didn't know what she expected him to reply, but his even, "Just that, Rachel," was flattening.

"That's hardly flattering," she tried to bring the lightness back into her voice and face, acutely conscious that Sandy was only a step away. The girl had moved into the sitting-room, but the door was wide open, and there was no movement from inside. She knew Sandy was probably standing there listening with interest.

Stephen said in a tone to match her own lightness, "I didn't know there was need for flattery between us, Rachel. Any more than the need to make an appointment ahead of time to see you. I've always thought friendship meant old slacks and face packs," he was chuckling again, "and dirty dishes in the sink, maybe, and no excuses given or needed, and no flattery in having to say things like, 'I was dying for the sight of you, Rachel, my treasure'," his voice fell to mockery again.

Keep it light, she thought. That was Stephen's motto. Keep it light and mocking and shallow, and never let the woman think it could be anything deeper and more lasting.

She decided that she simply wasn't in the mood for play-acting; that she was tired of the whole miserable situation; that she wasn't going to twist herself into knots over looking into blue eyes, into counting every laughter line in the suntanned features when he smiled, into the warm clasp of his hands over hers.

She said quietly, "Well I'm sorry, but I'm not in the mood for visitors tonight. For once I prefer to keep my dirty dishes — and now I remember the sink still has my breakfast things unwashed in it — and my old slacks and my curlers and face packs to myself. Also my coffee. Sorry, Stephen but," her tone was dryly mocking "friendship doesn't need fancy excuses for saying no, does it?"

"No," he said equably. "Right then, I'll scrounge some coffee at the radio office, and leave you in peace. I shan't even intrude over the air into your evening—there'll be no point in you listening in to my session tonight—I'm going to have to spin my time out of cobwebs and thin air."

"There's always the weather," she mocked.

"And I've fallen back on it before now," he reminded. "Snow in Birmingham, Ice in Bude, Heatwaves in Burma and Sandstorms in Zafaranboly . . . I can make positive drama out of it if I have to."

She couldn't resist the quick, "Where's Zafaranboly? Or did you just make that up?"

"Shame on you, girl—it's in Turkey. One day I might even turn up there to report a riot or minor war. If I do you'll know from the postcard that comes to adorn your mantelpiece."

"Don't bother to send it," she said quietly, "it'll only collect dust and I don't keep useless souvenirs. Goodnight, Stephen."

She knew that she'd almost said goodbye, not goodnight. She wished suddenly that she had, and had made him know she meant it. But at least she had told him not to send post-cards. She hoped that in the future he would remember it. She wanted nothing to remind her of him once he had gone. It was better to have the clean break rather than spend the future with one eye on the letter-box, hoping that some time he would remember and dash off a few lines.

She called, and knew her voice was too thin and sharp, "You've had time enough to scrub, Ann. Hop on out," then said to the open door of the sitting-room, "Sandy, I've written down the police number for you. Use it if you're the least bit worried."

The girl had been just inside the doorway, as Rachel had suspected. The thin face jerked into view and Sandy nodded.

"Don't you worry, Miss Penghill. Nothing's going to happen tonight. It's too wet. Even for a murder."

.   .   .

He had made his plans carefully and knew what he had to do. One stubby short finger went slowly down the columns of names in the directory till he finally discovered what he sought. His memory for names had always been good and the names of Clancy and Fergus and Egel were easily remembered, together with the numbers of the houses—all close to the Penghill place.

The scooter was slickly wet in the shadowed light of the distant street lamp when he left the call-box again. For a minute he thought the engine wasn't going to start and furiously he kicked at it, anger flaring in him again, then he gave a satisfied sigh. He moved off, rage giving way to ordered planning again.

The first thing was to look over the three houses and that of the Penghills. He had no intention now of going to the front door of the house and ringing the bell and letting the woman open the door. That way could spell disaster for him. If there was a chain on the door he wouldn't get in. She was unlikely to let him in on his own say-so, however convincingly he talked, if she was alone in the house with the child. Most likely the door would be slammed on him while she summoned the police and started screaming, rousing the child from sleep, and the whole street from Sunday night calm.

So she had to be lured out where a startled cry wouldn't be heard above the rain from the child's bedroom. She wasn't going to see him at all. He wasn't going to give her the chance. And she wasn't going to be able to talk tomorrow, or the next day, or the day after, of seeing him by the lake.

He had had a terrifying moment just before he had rung her and heard her voice again, when he had wondered if perhaps she had seen him and Rose together; whether both she and the child had done so and both were a danger to him. But when

71

panic had been fought down he had been certain that couldn't have happened. When he and Rose had arrived at the reserve there'd been no car parked on the road and there was nowhere else to park one. The woman and child had come later on and they hadn't ventured in as deeply, as far round the lake, as he and Rose. He had deliberately sought the most sheltered, most secluded place for himself and Rose to talk. And the scooter had been out of sight. He had done that deliberately for fear of some of the town youths coming along and finding it and taking it.

So only the woman was dangerous.

There was hate in him for her as he rode towards Acacia Way, going carefully on the wet slippery roads. In the whole journey he passed only one car and the driver never looked his way. He exulted in the fact that the very weather was helping him, that the very day with its settled calm and its dullness, was an ally.

He walked the last stretch of the way, the sodden stretch of jeans between oilskin and boot tops clinging to his legs in cold caress. He hardly noticed it. He was watching for the numbers on gate-posts, on front doors.

He came to the Egel place first and knew almost at once that it was no good to him. The whole place was shuttered up and in darkness. He knew, from the past times when an empty house was simply a place to be broken into with the mob he had been running with, what to look for and he gave a grunt of derision as his wet hands reached into the mail-box and came out clutching a little pile of envelopes. So much for the Egels, he thought contemptuously tossing the envelopes in a white flutter to join the draggle of leaves on the front lawn. They were away and advertising the fact to anyone who happened along, by not having their mail taken in by the neighbours.

He padded away down the wet footpath, eyes alert again for another number—the Clancy place. There was light here, at the back, and when he padded softly round the side of the place he gave a sign of satisfaction at the quick rattle of chain, and the sudden low warning growl.

So there was a dog. He decided not to bother with the Fergus place. He had what he wanted now—the name of a neighbour and the fact the neighbour had a dog that could get loose and stray.

He slid away before the dog could start in yapping and bring someone out, and went looking for the Penghill place. It was another glow of satisfaction that it was almost opposite the Clancy house—a smaller place than he'd expected from the size of the other houses in the street—but set on a fair-sized, tree-covered block.

There was light in one of the side rooms. He tried looking in, but there were no partly closed venetians as at the English house. There were holland blinds pulled down and curtains drawn across them as well.

There was no dog here though—another danger he had had to consider. The place was quiet except for the sound of a radio or television set somewhere inside. He went softly round the side of the place, pausing by the open garage doors and then slipping inside. There was no car, but the smell that told him plainly that one was normally kept there, which was what he had expected.

Penghill was absent, which was what he had been hoping for. It depended now on whether the man came back before the child was asleep, what steps he would take next. He had two means of getting the woman outside. If the man came back, the phone-call would tell the woman someone in the Clancy house was sick—asking the woman to come over—putting the receiver down before she started asking questions. The woman would leave the man in charge of the house and then go running out.

But he wouldn't give that story if she was alone. She wouldn't be likely to leave the child alone. She might ring another neighbour, explain and get the neighbour over to sit

73

there in case the child woke. And the neighbour could suggest she, the neighbour, went to the Clancy place instead. There were too many things could go wrong. So he'd use the story of the dog straying—ask her to go out and look in her yard to see if the dog was there.

That story wouldn't do though if the man was back. Then it would have to be the sickness one because if Penghill was back he wouldn't, would he, let the woman go out searching for the dog in the rain? He'd go himself surely.

So there were two stories and it depended on the man—on the unknown R. Penghill—which was to be used.

Either way the woman was going to come out. Into the rain. Into the darkness.

• • •

"All these years I've gone on and on at you," the thin tones had held a suffering burden of grief. "All these . . ."

"Give it away, mum." Rose's answering voice had been hoarse and tired and sick. Her thin fingers had been pressed against the livid bruises on her white skin. "I tell you I knew him. How was I t'know . . ."

"You didn't know him to speak to or you'd have known his name," Mrs. Gault had said pointedly. "You'd have known him someways better than just Mart."

"I knew he was at Spencers. I've seen him behind the counter. A real stick he looked." She had seen the stubborn grief settling down on to the lined face looking back at her and had gone on desperately, "Anyway we'd been introduced. All the sort of jazz you beef about. It was . . . Jim, I think it was. 'This is Mart' he says, and 'here's Rose' and that was that. What'd you expect? Us exchanging birth certificates and pedigrees?"

"If that's so . . ." Rose had seen the way the shame and worry had begun to slide out of the crumpled features and had begun to embroider the story in a husky dry whisper. There'd been sodas all round—there'd been quite a mob of them. And once Mart had been in the shop doorway when she'd gone by. He'd spoken to her, so when he'd stopped that day by her at the bus stop . . .

She let Mrs. Gault repeat it to Stephen Linquist, when he sat, his strong stock body a little hunched in the straight-backed chair by Rose's bed, and noted it all down.

He had been apologetic when Mrs. Gault had opened the door to him, explaining with the diffident, charming smile that had won stories out of harder types than the woman he faced, that a news tip had come from someone saying a police car had been at the Gault house and it was believed the daughter had had a serious accident. He had explained who he was, started to explain his radio news session and she had broken in quickly, "Oh I know you. I always listen in."

That was usually the way, and in a moment he had been inside and in another moment at Rose's bedside, while Mrs. Gault's thin, quavering voice had complained, "You can't do a thing here without the neighbours knowing. It'll be old Mrs. Vaughan in number thirty who rung you, wouldn't it be? She sits at her front window all the time, just watching."

"I don't know who it was," he told them, to be met by Rose's shrewd, husky-voiced:

"News tips're paid for."

"So are interviews, sometimes," he reminded. "It depends on the sort of story I get."

"The police said we weren't to let it out," Mrs. Gault protested wearily. "Keep quiet they told us, or he might run off. The man who . . ."

"Wouldn't you say he's disappeared already?" Stephen suggested.

"*They* don't think so. They reckon he thinks he killed Rose. Else he wouldn't have thrown her into the lake that way."

Stephen had no compunction in leading them on. He knew the girl wanted to talk, that already she was picturing herself a

75

celebrity. All that was necessary was to sift the fact from the fancy.

He went to Giddings for that and the sergeant swore forcibly and at length.

"I didn't use my loaf," he admitted grudgingly at last. "I warned the farm chap who brought back Rose to keep quiet about it all, but I forgot the neighbours. All right, you have it, but it's not to be used. No, I'm not giving you his second name either, and yes," he went on impatiently, "I know you can go to Spencers' owner and get the name, but remember I can jump on you if you don't play ball. You can use the whole story in the morning, whether he's back or not. If the latter, we'll know he's running. For the moment I expect him to land home and save us a lot of trouble.

"I'll tell you this anyway—it's not the high drama Mrs. Gault's little Rose tells you. It's just a sorry little tale of a girl picking up someone who didn't know her from Eve. There's something for your session—I'll give you some data if you like about the number of kids who've landed into trouble that way. You can run the cases without mentioning this one. It might lead some of the little fools to think twice, if they're listening to you and not out having a necking session with something picked up already."

"The girl has it she knew him to speak to—that . . ."

"By the time she gets into court they'll have swapped rattles in the cradle," Giddings derided. "But you can't use the story tonight—anyway you couldn't do an interview with her over the air tonight in any case, though she'd relish it, damn her. But I'll tell you something you can talk about—ask for anyone —no reason and that face might bring someone forward out of curiosity—who was in the reserve, by the lake, today, to give us or you a ring. I want a witness who saw Rose and the boy together if I can get one."

"That's all the meat you're going to give me to cook up?" Stephen protesed.

"Knowing you I bet the result'll be a feast, but here's another trifle for you—a prowler. That's always good for a few shudders."

·   ·   ·

He had nearly forgotten that the last of the coins from Ivy's rice caddy were gone. Only when he had sighted the call-box, exulting in his closeness to the Penghill house and the fact that he could keep the place under observation while he phoned, did he remember about the coins. He had to go back to the scooter, cursing, and ride back to the shopping centre, cruising along till he found something open in the Sunday silence. It was a milk-bar and because he was afraid of being refused the coins if he simply asked for change, he was forced to buy a coke and stand there, drinking it, while the elderly man behind the counter talked of the weather.

His mind was on the phone-call, on the fact that the woman would have to find something to throw over her before she went outdoors, giving him time to get from the call-box into the Penghill grounds again. The man's thick slow voice penetrated only vaguely, but suddenly Mart jerked into a violent, "What's funny about it? What're you getting at, eh?"

The red-veined faded eyes had a shocked dazed look as they gazed back at him. "I only said it was funny you're out in this deluge. I was just wonderin' . . ."

Mart croaked a laugh into the silence. He was furious with himself for the slip, for the sudden burst of panic-stricken anger. Now the little man was going to remember him. Then he told himself it didn't matter. It didn't matter at all that he should be seen tonight in a run-down milk-bar. The fact wasn't going to connect him up with the woman in the Penghill place. Was it? Or with Rose? And the lake?

He went out without saying anything, and kicked the scooter into life, cruising back towards Acacia Way. When he padded slowly into the Penghill place again, the car was still out and the garage still empty and the light was still on in

77

the side room, with the wireless or television still going.

The clock in the milk-bar had said nearly nine when he'd left the place. He wondered, standing just inside the shelter of the garage, prepared to dodge round the side of it if a car turned into the street, if the child would be already in bed. Then he decided to wait. He told himself over and over that there was no hurry. If the man came back or not his plans were still ready. Far better to wait to make sure the child was out of the way, so that she wouldn't rush out instead of the woman to look for the non-existent dog.

It was nearly half past nine by the luminous hands of his watch when he made a move. The garage was still empty and the street lay wet and silent, shadows made blacker by the few widely spaced street lights as he padded over to the call-box and slipped inside.

He had no need to look up the number. He'd memorised it from the first time. His finger was right, slow-moving, as he worked it in the dial and waited.

Fury built up in him when all that answered was the engaged signal.

He had to fight down rising panic, the frightened conviction that the woman had simply taken the receiver off the hook and was going to leave it off all evening to save being disturbed; that his plans were going to be abortive and he would, after all, have to go up to the house itself and knock and bring her to the door; before there was finally a breathlessly faint, "Hello."

The words tumbled out of him in sheer overwhelming relief and afterwards he was glad it had happened like that because it gave her no time to break in and try to question him and maybe trip him up and make her suspicious.

He got out rapidly, "Mrs. Penghill, this is Clancys from over the way. Our dog's ill and has got out and we're worried sick and I'm trying to find it and I thought maybe it's slipped into somebody's garage for shelter and I just wondered if you'd be so good as to go look. I wouldn't ask on a night like this, but with it being ill . . ."

He went on, drowning out any attempt she might have made to break in, telling her over and over that the dog was seriously ill and might be in real trouble, thanking her, ringing off before she could possibly suggest that somebody from the Clancy place come right over and make a thorough search for the brute.

He was shaking, sweating, when he finally rang off and padded back across the shadows into the Penghill grounds, into the open garage, behind the concertina shadows of the folding doors. Standing there he could picture her inside, angry and impatient at having to do the neighbourly service, searching for something to throw over herself, perhaps looking in on the child to make sure the sound of the ringing phone hadn't disturbed her.

Then he saw the sudden shaft of light spring out from the back of the house; light that was immediately darkened by the shadow of someone slipping out. He heard the rapid thud-thud of feet on the path, then someone dashed into the shelter of the garage.

His hands were ready and out-thrust, reaching greedily, savagely.

CHAPTER SEVEN

THERE was only one drawback to the new premises in Provence Street. Because the shop and the flat above it stood at the end of the long row of shops, there was no parking space, no driveway into the back of her place, and no garage. Rachel had been forced from necessity to rent a garage at the far end of the street. It was never pleasant, at night, to walk through the deserted, shadowed stretch of street to her own premises. It was, she decided, throwing open the door and rushing in against the pull and pressure of the rain-drenched wind, discomfort almost beyond bearing on a night like the present one.

She went up the treads of the old staircase, resolving that something would have to be done about it as soon as funds permitted. Because the old premises stood next to a narrow dirt-paved lane, it would, she decided, be possible to use that as a driveway into the back of her place if a garage could somehow be squeezed into the tiny area at the back of the shop.

There would be, she thought, thankfully throwing off clothes that had become damp just in her brief journey on foot, a chance to discuss the idea of the garage tomorrow. Old Mr. Timson, who had been the town's oldest handyman for as long as she could remember, was due in the morning to fix the old stairs. If she drew him an idea of what she meant he might have some suggestions of his own to make.

Going into the small sitting-room that overlooked Provence Street she lit the gas fire, curling up in front of it, reaching for cigarettes and concentrating her thoughts on the coming week —willing herself to throw over the depression that had been steadily clamping down on her ever since Stephen's call. She listed silently all that had to be done to make sure that the announcement in the window "Opening on the 17th" would happen on oiled springs. One week, she reflected. Not long for final jewellery stock to arrive, for her to attend two exhibitions, for Timson to attend to the stairs, for the display cases to be filled and a dozen and one other trifles to be seen to.

She began jotting down the items, feeling tiredness sweeping over her at the prospect of it all, but she knew as she wrote that all of it, tiredness or not, was going to ease her over the time between now and Stephen's going and that she should grasp at it all thankfully.

Thinking again of Stephen brought anger. In a burst of temper against him and against fate and her own emotions she jumped to her feet. He wasn't going to break in on her any more that night, she told herself. She went running across the small room, flicking the portable radio from its shelf and putting it away in the fireplace cupboard, turning the key on it and tossing the key into a vase on the table. Now, if the temptation to hear his voice again at ten-thirty overwhelmed her she would have second thoughts before she got the radio out. Standing there, she thought suddenly, 'And he's not going to reach me on the phone either', and she went down into the coldness of the showroom to take the receiver from the hook and leave it there, blank and black on the white painted table.

·   ·   ·

Sandy Micklin was chewing her nails, oblivious to the damage to the polish she had been at pains to put on them only that afternoon, wondering what Mrs. Penghill would say, and do. Not that it mattered, she decided finally. There were plenty of jobs going for sitters—you just had to offer and people fell over themselves to grab you. And besides . . . considering what had happened . .

The trouble was she didn't know if she would be believed.

After all, what was there in it? A shadow and the driving rain and a yell that could have been the cat's, and there was only her own word for it and Mrs. Penghill could easily claim it was all a trumped-up story to have Lloyd in the house, where he'd been forbidden to go.

True, there was the cat. She eyed him pensively where he sat in front of the fire. His blue eyes still looked dark-irised and jungle wild and she knew if she put down her hand she would feel the fur, not sleek to his fat body as usual, but slightly raised as though at any minute he would become again a creature of spitting, screeching fury.

But the cat couldn't talk. And anyway anyone knew that the Siamese cats were highly strung and jumped at shadows. Mrs. Penghill herself was always saying so and saying what an awful shrieking cry they had into the bargain. Mrs. Penghill didn't, Sandy had often considered, really like the cat at all, but Ann doted on it.

She said to the Siamese, "What was out there?" then both of them jumped as the phone rang. The cat yowled, taking one flying leap to her shoulder, draping herself about her neck as it had done before. She knew it was no use trying to dislodge it, and the feel of its warmth was comforting as she went out into the hall.

When she had come back inside she had switched on all the lights against the shadows in the house. That would be another cause for complaint when Mrs. Penghill came back, she thought ruefully.

She said into the receiver "Hello" and the voice said briskly, "Is that you again, Miss Penghill?"

"No it isn't. Miss Penghill's gone home. This is Mrs. Penghill's sitter."

"Sandy?" The voice sharpened, going on before she could answer, "This is Mrs. Swan from down the road."

She murmured, "Yes, Mrs. Swan," and waited, one hand reaching up to the cat's warm body.

"Did Miss Penghill say something to you about me ringing a while back—earlier this evening?"

"Oh yes." Fright was sweeping back. She looked into the hall mirror and saw her eyes big and round and drowned in fright. She said huskily, "Yes, I forgot about that . . . I mean . . . you rang and said . . ."

"So you know. Well I wanted to speak to Miss Penghill, but . . . when Mrs. Penghill comes in tell her about it and tell her I've been ringing other mothers and one of them says her neighbour—in Fielding Street that is—has had a prowler. Now don't get upset, Sandy, they're two streets away . . . but this Mrs. English heard a crashing noise and looked out. She couldn't see anything, but she was frightened for fear something had broken up in the storm. She went out a bit later with a torch and there were footprints, men's footprints, in the wet ground all under the trees round the side of the house. And she has a daughter, like us. The police came and looked round, but nobody's been picked up so far as I know. But tell Mrs. Penghill when she comes in, will you? Sandy!" her voice sharpened. "Sandy!" Are you still there?"

"Mrs. Swan, I'm scared." Sandy's voice was so thick with fright it startled even herself. "I went out—just a little while back. To the garage. Mrs. Swan, I had the Siamese cat on my shoulder—round my neck. He jumps at you. He doesn't mean a scrap of harm, but you can't pry him loose, so I went out with him round my neck because I thought he'd soon jump off when he felt the wind. Only he didn't. I should've thought he wouldn't want to get his feet wet. And Mrs. Swan . . . I think there was someone in the garage. I'm not making it up!" her voice wavered in desperation. "Something happened—I heard something move, but the cat seemed to heave up and then there was a terrible screaming and when he jumped off that way I tripped someway and I fell. Mrs. Swan, I know the cat was yowling, but I thought someone screamed—a person— and then . . . the cat kept spitting and yowling and there was

83

the noise of the storm, but I'm sure someone was running . . . away. I came right on in . . ."

"Have you rung the police?"

"I was scared to, Mrs. Swan. I thought Mrs. Penghill mightn't believe me and *they* wouldn't either and anyway the first thing I thought of doing was telling my Lloyd and I rang him and he said he was coming over to stay with me no matter what Mrs. P'd say. I was waiting when you rang."

"Sandy, you get on to the police!" the voice was shrill. "You get on to them this minute. You hear?"

•   •   •

Three long raking scratches down the side of his face was a smarting, bleeding reminder of bitter failure, of panic, of running away, of botching the whole thing. His crash helmet had saved him from the full onslaught of the heavy, yowling avalanche that had heaved up from the woman's shoulder to meet his outstretched hands, springing upwards at his head and shoulders, falling heavily downwards after raking him, still yowling.

He had seen the shadowy figure of the woman falling downwards and forwards away from him; had seen the glow of cat's eyes and had panicked. The rage in him was so violent a thing his whole body was shaking. There was rage at the woman, at the cat, at himself, at his failure, at the cold, burning knowledge that if he hadn't panicked and run the way he had he could still have settled with the woman.

A kick—one good hard kick with his boot—would have sent the cat yowling and flying for safety. Wouldn't it have? And the woman had been on the ground. Hadn't she? She would have been at a disadvantage, on her hands and knees, easy for him to knock flat, to deal with.

And instead he had let panic and pain take over and he had fled the place. And afterwards, sick with fear and bitterness, he had seen light after light come on till the house was a beacon in the darkened, rain-swept street.

He hadn't dared hang round. He had imagined her at the phone, ringing the police, gasping out her story, looking for some weapon, waiting panic-eyed and hand at her throat, close to the child, till help came. He had known that he wouldn't, no matter what story he spun, get her out that night.

Which left breaking in. Getting to her in the silent house somewhere, in the night. And that would only be possible, wouldn't it, if the police didn't stay, if the man . . . if the unknown R. Penghill . . . didn't return.

He had swept away on the scooter, riding violently, too fast, through the streets, out into the open roads beyond the town, trying to still the panic, the sense of failure, trying to think.

It was difficult, growing more difficult all the time, to remember Rose. When he did so it was to remember she was unlikely to be found till the morning. So he still had time. That thought calmed him and helped him. While there was time there was hope. He nearly laughed at the cliché. It reminded him of Ivy, in her depressed moments, saying slowly, "While there's life there's hope of better things. Just you remember that. While there's life there's a chance to turn over a new leaf."

The remembrance made him angry again. He didn't want to think of Ivy. It was because of her and Rose and the woman in the Penghill house that he was riding through the rain-drenched night. The whole thing was their fault. If Rose hadn't been there the way she had been; if she hadn't laughed; if Ivy didn't know all about the past; if the woman hadn't seen him . . .

But there was still time. The thought came back as sweet relief to his tortured mind. Rose wouldn't be found till the morning. The news wouldn't be broadcast, in the papers, till mid-day at least. So the woman wouldn't know. And in the morning she'd be alone. Wouldn't she? The man would have gone to work and the child to school and the woman wouldn't be behind locked doors. Not in daylight. Not when the baker, the postman, the milkman and all the rest of a workaday world, would be coming along.

But in the morning he might be seen. In the morning he was supposed to be at work himself. What if, when the woman was later found, they looked for someone who wasn't at his usual place of work? What if they went to his home and asked Ivy if he'd been home? And told her why they were asking. What if Ivy put two and two together?

He knew then that someway, if it was at all possible, he had to deal with the woman that night.

He had circled round the town by then, swept back into it, down the cold, almost deserted stretch of shopping centre, past Spencers, past the milk-bar where he'd been earlier. It was shuttered and dark now, and so was the supermarket and the shining new butchery, and the beauty salon with its pink and gold front. So was the Chinese café and the place next door with the flaring red streamers across the window, "Opening on the 17th".

Slowly he lugged towards Acacia Way again, urgency to find out what was happening over-riding the caution, the fear, that urged him to keep away. But it was a free country, he told himself. Nothing to say he was connected with what had happened at the Penghill place.

Expectant as he was, the sight of the street brought back panic. He saw the lights in nearly every house, saw the faces at windows behind pulled-back curtains. He saw people who had even braved the cold and wind to come out on front porches to stare. He wondered, seeing the police car outside the Penghill place, how long it would be before the night quietened down again

There were two boys, oilskin-clad, sharing a huge mush-rooming black umbrella, near the police car, gazing with interest at the house. He let the scooter slide to a standstill, because there was no reason why a passer-by couldn't stop to question what was going on. Was there? In fact if he had passed by, he thought suddenly, without a second look that might have seemed queer to watchers.

He asked huskily, "What's cooking?" and saw the two night-pale faces turning towards him.

They were about thirteen or fourteen he thought. And almost rigid with cold and excitement.

One of them burst out, "A girl got attacked in there. Right in that place. See? She was sitting with the kid in there'n come on out for somethin' and someone whacked her brains out."

He nearly laughed. He said instead, "Who sent for the police then?"

"She did. She . . ."

"What?" He was jeering at them, laughter bubbling in him at the absurdity of it all, "With her brains whacked out?"

The two of them started to snigger in great gulps. The second of them, in a voice that was breaking raggedly said quickly, "She just got a fright I reckon. Some other dame round here flipped her lid. She was ringing my old woman a while back and talking about men being nasty to her kid and my old lady was flapping about my sister. I reckon," he nodded sagely, "there's nothing in it. This," he waved his hand to the lighted house, "I bet the sitter heard and got a scare out of a shadow . . ."

"Aren't the Penghills home?"

"No. You know 'em?" The boy didn't wait for an answer. "Been out all day. *His* sister was there a while back. I know because the old flap that rung my old lady said she'd rung Miss Penghill here a while back. I guess she went off home'n . . ."

He wasn't listening. He was kicking the scooter into life, exultation in him. He said huskily, "Well, it's nothing to do with me. Is it? I'll be off."

They said something, but he still wasn't listening. All he could think of were the words, "His sister was there a while back. The old flap . . . rung Miss Penghill . . ."

Miss Penghill. Not Mrs. R. Penghill at all. *She'd* been away all day. It was Miss Penghill. He remembered the likeness of the child and the woman. That had fooled him. But it was the aunt he wanted. Not the mother. And she didn't live there. She lived somewhere else.

On her own?

. . .

Sandy was torn between sheer excitement, fright and a feeling that at any minute her stomach would simply cease being a controlled part of her and disgrace her utterly. She had faced the police and told her story twice. They had written it down, but hadn't said whether they believed her or not. They had gone out though and searched the garage and the grounds, then come back in to tell her to lock up securely, not to let anyone in and to ring again if anything happened.

And to get Mr. and Mrs. Penghill back home.

She had tried to do that, but when she had rung the number they'd left for her she was told they'd already left the house there and must be on their way back.

She explained that to Stephen Linquist, who arrived as the police were leaving. The constable who had taken down her story told her who he was, but she hadn't needed the introduction.

She explained, "But I know Mr. Linquist because he's been here with Miss Penghill."

"And that makes us friends, doesn't it, Sandy?"

His smile was warm and disarming. "May I come in? And ask questions?"

"She's answered enough questions to fill a bleeding barrel." That was Lloyd, who had arrived in the middle of the police questioning to sit darkly glowering on the edge of a chair, his big hands linked tightly between the knees of his tight grey slacks.

Stephen looked across at the young giant whose curly blue-black hair glistened wetly under the electric light. He looked into the black-browed scowl over the deep-set grey eyes and offered cigarettes with a quiet, "Just as well she's capable of answering them, isn't it, Lloyd?"

Sandy gasped. She merely gulped silently when Stephen, holding a lighter to the younger man's cigarette, asked in the same pleasant, diffident voice, "Would you say, Sandy, that the cat yowled and jumped off your shoulder because it was touched? Because someone had reached out for you?"

"You're scaring her black-gutted!" Lloyd pointed out. "She hasn't got to answer questions from you."

"Of course not." Stephen rose to his feet. Half turning towards the door he said, as though he'd already lost interest, "If you don't feel like talking, Sandy, I'll be off."

Sandy's voice came back. She could see her chance of being in the limelight sliding away. She threw a look of disgust at Lloyd, a quick, "I don't mind talking, Mr. Linquist," at the older man and pushed a chair forwards for him towards the fire, waiting till he had settled his broad, stocky body, before she started, "It was this way."

He listened critically, though to the young pair he seemed almost disinterested, sitting with straddled, outflung legs and eyes half closed. It was a pose he had learned from long experience made those he interviewed say far more than they had intended. Sandy was no exception. The only thing was he didn't know, as he had done with Rose Gault, which was fact and which fiction.

And there was no Giddings this time to tell him.

He said at last, "So Rachel Penghill was here and told you about Mrs. Swan ringing up in a panic. Didn't Miss Penghill maybe say that Lloyd should come on over and sit with you?"

His half closed eyes noted the way her young too-red mouth pouted.

"No, she didn't." Her tone was resentful. "I asked that myself and she jumped at me. Mrs. Penghill, see, makes it a rule I don't have boys round, though Lloyd'n me're . . ."

"Yes. So Rachel vetoed Lloyd coming round." He was rising to his feet.

He felt that the whole story rested on that—in a teenager's urge to have her boy friend in for a quiet necking session without getting into trouble about it. Easy enough to think up a prowler as an excuse when you'd already been warned that there was a phone nuisance round the area. Probably, he thought cynically, shrugging into his overcoat, saying goodnight to the pair of them in the hall, she had intended when Mrs. Penghill got home and found them to say someone had actually rung. Then on Mrs. Swan's second call she had jumped at the Fielding Street story and invented a prowler.

And the thing had got out of hand. She hadn't been able to take back the words and had had to ring the police. And then she had gone on embroidering.

He'd ring Rachel, he thought suddenly. Probably, in spite of him telling her not to bother with his session that evening she'd listen in. And hear the story of the prowler at Penghills' and become alarmed. He'd ring her first and tell her his idea.

But when he called her number, twice, and each time heard only the engaged signal, he decided to let it go.

CHAPTER EIGHT

His first exultation had given way to irritation and then to rage, when he had realised he was as far from finding her as ever, because there was no other Penghill in the directory except for the one on Acacia Way. He should have remembered that, he chided himself. He had noticed before there was only that one entry under the name. And he'd forgotten.

He should have asked the two boys, he reflected. He should have said, when they'd spoken of Miss Penghill going home, "And where's that?"

And then panic had come back, to be swept away in the relief of knowing that he hadn't made that mistake. Because if he had asked they might have remembered, and remembered his face. Mightn't they? And afterwards . . . they might have told the police about him. Mightn't they? They must have seen him fairly clearly in the lights from the police car.

He stood there in the call-box in which he seemed now to have spent half a lifetime, swearing, reflecting on the chasm into which he had nearly fallen, worrying over the fact that the two of them had seen him, frightened that it might somehow connect him with what was going to happen, with what had happened before.

But it couldn't he decided, at last. He'd been a passer-by who'd seen the lights, the police car, the boys, and had simply pulled up out of idle curiosity.

But it still didn't get him any further towards finding the woman. She was somewhere there in the dark, maybe close to him, maybe some distance away, but as dangerous to his safety as ever.

Then it came to him. He fingered coins nervously and wondered if the Penghill house would be quiet again by now. Then he told himself that it didn't matter one way or the other.

What did it matter if a friend phoned and asked if Miss Penghill was there, and when told no, asked for her phone number, her address—saying perhaps, that they were someone passing through who'd lost her address?

They wouldn't think anything of that. Would they?

．　　　．　　　．

Ann hunched under the covers of the small narrow bed, wakeful, alert for sounds from outside. She had woken when the police had come. One of them, young and smiling, had looked in on her, told her not to worry, to be a good girl and go back to sleep because everything was all right.

But she hadn't believed that. Not after listening, wide-eyed and shivering, out in the hall, while Sandy talked to Stephen Linquist.

She lay there trying to imagine what it would feel like to go out into the cold, windy darkness and know there was someone else there, silent and motionless at your side, and then to feel reaching hands coming out towards you.

There was a feeling of delicious horror and excitement all through her, keeping her wakeful. She wished that Sandy had pulled down the blind again over the window, but it was up and there was a pale square there in the black darkness of the wall that was terrifying because she could imagine it suddenly filling with a face—a white, staring face and groping hands.

She was wondering if she had the gumption to slide out of bed, take a running jump at the shade and pull it clattering down to shut out the lighted square, when she heard the dog somewhere outside.

There was a burst of quick, excited barking, then a long drawn howl and more sharp barking. As though it was in pain,

Ann reflected. Then imagination jumped at her like a figure in the night, telling her that it was as though the animal had maybe been kicked aside.

She slid from the bed, shivering, pattering towards the door. Sandy, she reflected wistfully, couldn't be mad if she begged to sit by the fire till she was sleepy again. She opened the door a crack and then she could hear Sandy saying in a high excited voice:

"I clean forgot all about it. Can you just imagine that, Lloyd? I forgot all about it!"

"Well what's it matter?"

"Well they asked, didn't they? And the dog's sick—it's a prize collie—and Mrs. Clancy was terribly kind that time Mrs. Penghill was ill for weeks. I just know that if Mrs. P was home she'd . . ."

"You mean you want to go out and look-see if the howling brute's theirs?" Lloyd sounded incredulous.

"*You're* here, aren't you?" was the reasonable retort.

"And very comfortable, too, ta."

"Oh Lloyd," her tone was wheedling now, "it's just a matter of stepping out. And he wouldn't be round now, after the police being here and all. You've only got to go and look—she sounds out near the back fence. Of course," her tone was suddenly far too casual, "if you're scared silly of stepping out . . ."

"Who says so? All right, I'll go if you come too. You know the brute you said and I'm not going to have my fingers nipped off. A sick dog's a cranky one—you can whistle it in if it's theirs."

Ann could hear them talking, arguing, going towards the back of the house. She heard Sandy squealing about the sudden buffeting of cold and wind from outside. Ann could feel it herself coming through the house from the open doorway.

When the phone rang she just stood there. She could see it from her bedroom doorway. The impatient sound of the ringing seemed to fill the narrow space. When Sandy and Lloyd didn't come back she went pattering, bare-footed, across the carpet.

She had quite forgotten Rachel's insistence on her not answering the phone. She said, her small voice precise, remembering the many lessons Roger Penghill had drilled into her. "This is the Penghill house—Ann speaking."

The voice sounded far away. It asked, "Is Miss Penghill there?"

She said quickly, "Oh no, she's gone home."

"Would you give me the address, Ann?" the voice was clearer now. "I'm passing through and I've mislaid it and wanted to . . ."

Someone I knew, she thought, and tried to put a name to the voice but failed, while she said helpfully, "It's the last shop in Provence Street, next to the lane. And next to Wing Lee's café on the other side."

She didn't as she was thanked, wonder why the address had been mislaid. Rachel had only just moved to the new place. It was quite quite reasonable that one of her out-of-town friends or customers had forgotten where the new place was.

With the receiver back in place, her bedroom yawned dark and cold behind her because she hadn't put on the light when she had slipped out of bed. Looking at the black yawning gap in the wall she knew she wasn't going back into the bedroom by herself. She was going to sit by the fire till Sandy and Lloyd came back, and then she would somehow make Sandy go into the dark bedroom with her and pull down the shade over the window and keep all the fright of the night away from her.

It was cold there in the hall without her dressing-gown— with just the pink flowered white pyjamas over her shivering body, but the electric fire was warm and she pulled the biggest of the easy chairs over to it and curled up there, arms curved round her hunched-up knees, ears alert for odd sounds that could mean more trouble.

94

When the back door crashed shut and footsteps came in she cowered and sat waiting, but they didn't come into the room. Instead there was the sound of high-pitched giggling and Sandy's shrieked, "Don't you dare!" and more giggling and Lloyd talking in a deep mocking voice.

The night was suddenly a thing of embarrassment and because she didn't want to listen to the giggling and the voices she leaned forwards and switched on the radio, letting the music engulf the noises from the back of the house. But Sandy and Lloyd had heard it start up and almost immediately Sandy was there in the doorway. Her face was unnaturally red and she looked cross, her voice terse when she said, "What do you think *you're* up to?"

"Sitting," Ann told her solemnly," and listening."

"That's it, kiddo." Lloyd's snort of laughter was loud. "You tell the truth and she can't whack you for fibbin'. Sitting and listening, that's it to a T, but aren't you supposed to be lying down and sleeping, kiddo?"

"My name's Ann," she told him equably. "And I can't go to sleep because of all the noise and . . ."

"She's scared," Lloyd said. "Kiddo's scared, Sandy. She wants us to hold her little hand," but in spite of the mockery in his voice there was kindness in the sudden touch of his big hand over hers.

"Oh let her stay up," Sandy flopped into the other easy chair. "Nothing's normal about tonight, not even dogs. Any normal mutt'd've come rushing when we called and been wagging its backside over getting into the warm, but what does the crazy brute do but hide." Then her voice went up in excitement, "Lloyd, listen! We're getting in the news . . ."

The three of them hunched there while Stephen spoke of the night's prowlers and scares. Ann stole a glimpse of Sandy's face and saw the small white teeth clenched into the full lower lip and Lloyd's oil-bright dark eyes glistening, his mouth curving into a smile that had nothing to do with amusement.

They were sitting like that, rigid with the knowledge that it was themselves, and the Penghill house, that was being discussed, when the dog began barking again long howls mingled with savage loud barking.

Sandy jumped up in exasperation, "I'll get it this time! I will! Lloyd, you just come and hold the torch and I'll get it this time."

She went running out and reluctantly Lloyd rose, too, but he went on standing there for a full two minutes, apparently lost in the sound of Stephen's quiet voice, before Sandy came running back, demanding that he wake up and follow her, just as Ann was turning, just as her eyes were taking on a shiny bright look of anticipation, just as her mouth opened to say, "*I* was there. I was by the lake today."

She said it instead to the empty room. She said it again to the radio, as though Stephen was there and could hear her. The danger had suddenly gone out of the night and there was anticipation instead, the anticipation of something exciting. Her thoughts made no attempt to grabble with wondering why she was being asked to come forward. It was enough that now she had a chance to be, like Sandy, in the full glare of limelight.

After another minute, impatient at the slow deep voice speaking only of things that bored her; of girls who were silly enough to pick up young men they didn't know, she went out into the hall again. The door of her bedroom still gaped blackly and she was afraid again, angling the receiver of the phone as she picked it up so that she didn't have to stand with her back to the gaping blackness.

But she couldn't remember the number of the radio station and she had to put down the receiver again while she searched the directory.

She was dialling the second of the numbers when Sandy came running back. She demanded, "What are you doing?" And then, her voice going up in indignation, she cried, "You put that phone down, Ann Penghill! You put it down this minute! You know you're not allowed to go to the phone. Your Aunt told me. She told me, too, so you needn't shake your head, Ann Penghill. You put it down."

"I was only going to ring someone up," Ann protested.

"At this hour of the night? You gone crackers, kiddo?" That was Lloyd, hovering giant-like and black-browed at the back of the hall, "All your pals will be in bed like good little girls by this time."

"And anyway I want to ring Mrs. Clancy, so give." Sandy held out an imperative hand for the phone. "That silly mutt just won't come, so maybe if Mrs. C comes on over they can cope with it."

She was dialling rapidly, her voice still high and shrill when she said into the black mouthpiece, "Mrs. Clancy, I'm just sure your dog's out back right now, but it won't come to me and Lloyd and it's just soaking out there so if you'd come on over . . . what?" Ann saw the strange way Sandy's face was working, and the way it was changing expression. She pressed backwards, suddenly frightened, and found herself up against Lloyd's hard body. She didn't mind. It was suddenly comforting, because Sandy was crying, "But Mrs. Clancy, you rung me. You must've, because I went on out . . ." and then she let the receiver fall. Her eyes were frightened circles in her white face. "She never called me at all. It was all a lie. It was *him*. It was him called me and made me go out there. Lloyd, it was *him* . . ."

．　　　．　　　．

His leather-gauntleted hands beat gently one into another as he stood in the narrow laneway at the side of the shop, looking up at the square of light from the window in the upper storey. He hadn't worn the gloves in the garage at the Penghill place— there he had wanted his hands free and uncumbered. Here he had taken them from the little tool-box on the back of the scooter and slipped his hands into them because he was

97　　　　　　　　　　UN—G

considering the possibilities of breaking-in and he had thought of the risk of fingerprints.

There had been fury in him again when he had come down the street of closed and shuttered shops, realising that twice at least that night he had swept past the woman's home and never known it.

He had circled round and up and down the street twice, riding slowly by, his gaze watchful through the driving rain, noting the red signs slashing the window that informed passers-by that the place wouldn't be opening until the seventeenth. Then he had left the scooter well away from the place and come padding back, going past the premises twice, gaze still alert, anger building up because the sign-writers had not yet painted the phone number on the window.

He had known then that he couldn't ring her and bring her down to the door on some trumped-up excuse, to let him safely inside the place, because she wouldn't be listed in the phone directory yet. He remembered day by day, in the past few weeks, passing the place while it was slowly changed from the closed and shuttered emptiness that it had held for as long as he had been in the town. There was no help for him in the remembrance. If the place had been occupied before he would have remembered, been able to search the directory for the former tenant's name, and find the phone number. But it had been empty too long and her name wasn't listed. Which left him with two alternatives — break in when the place was quiet, or bring her to the door and chance there being a chain to hold it against him and a frightened refusal to remove.

He wondered, one hand still gently moulding into the palm of the other, whether the sitter at Penghill's house had rung the woman already. If that had happened, was the woman on guard now? Alert to jump at shadows?

It took him a slow twenty minutes before he had closely considered the idea of breaking-in and reluctantly, angrily, decided against it. There were bars across the tiny window downstairs on to the laneway, and bars also against the upstairs windows. It would be sheer lunacy to try and saw through them or try to force them out of their foundations. Even on a night like the present one someone could come and see them; or the woman could hear him. And if the sitter had rung her and she was alert . . . he had told himself it was madness even to think of the idea.

That left the tempting polished glass of the window. It seemed so easy to cut through it, to slide a hand in and open the door and get inside. But the very temptation warned him to be careful. If there were bars on the windows there was almost certainly a burglar alarm. Almost definitely one when he considered the place was being remodelled as a jewellery store.

Slowly he pulled off the gauntlets, thrusting them inside the jumper under his oilskin. They struck cold and clammy against his shirt front, but he barely noticed it. He was concentrating on the fact that the only way he could reach her was by bringing her down and forcing her somehow, someway to open the door, and let him in.

But why would she let a stranger into her home? When she was alone and the whole street was closed and dark and quiet?

It was when his gaze saw the golden-painted chinese characters on Wing Lee's window that he started to laugh. The sound came bubbling up into his throat, forcing out between his lips, because the answer had been there all along.

He went quite confidently up to her door and reached up towards the little white-capped press button at the side of it. He wondered, standing there with the cold wind whipping at the sodden stretch of jeans between oilskin hem and boot tops, what she was thinking as she heard the bell.

It took her a long time to answer. He'd pressed the bell three times, urgently, because it didn't matter how much he continued to ring, considering what he was going to say, before a light came on over the doorway and then bolts slid back and the door opened—a crack. As he had feared there was a chain, a thick heavy one he noted in one sweeping glance before he burst out, "There's something burning! Next door. I can smell it and I saw your lights . . ."

The chain rattled and fell away. She was starting forwards, ready to come out and smell for herself, anxiety plain on her pale face, when he thrust her backwards, speaking rapidly, urgently, to stop her from crying out, from guessing why he was there, "Get to the phone, can't you? Quick! The whole block'll go up if there's a fire, if . . ."

He was kicking the door shut behind him, one hand in the pocket of his coat. He said, staring into her startled eyes, "I've a gun. You understand me?" and was furious because his voice was so high and cracked, as shrill as a woman's. "Go on. Get back," he told her in the same shrill voice that he couldn't control

She went slowly, watchful gaze on his face. Her own face was expressionless, her hands outspread to prevent herself from bumping into anything, though the place—the showroom he realised—was empty except for a long counter against the side wall.

He knew what he was going to do. He was going to force her back to the stairs and then make her turn round to go up them. And as soon as she turned he was going to take his hand from his pocket—not with a gun, but with the jemmy from his tool-box, and bring it down on the back of her head. And then he was going to . . .

Then in sick rising panic, looking into the steady gaze fixed on his, he knew he wasn't going to do any of it. That he couldn't. That he could no more strike her down than he could stand here and cut his own throat. The thought of it—of hitting her, of a gush of blood, of standing over her and finishing her off . . . was a rising gorge of sickness in his throat, making him retch aloud.

Fury burned in him for that, and for the woman actually

seeing the disgrace of it. He wanted to scream at her, but he couldn't get any words out and he had the feeling that she knew exactly what he was feeling and thinking and was contemptuous. Just that and nothing more. Contemptuous. Not even afraid of him.

But he had to get rid of her, he reminded himself desperately. Hadn't he plotted and planned all the night since they had first met, to get rid of her? Hadn't he worked out that she could send him to prison? That she was a danger to his liberty?

The sickness was washed away in another panic altogether, the knowledge that now she had seen him face to face, in a clear light, and that even if he went away she could now ring the police, give a good description of him and tell them he had broken in and threatened her.

Then she jerked, "I've seen you before," and it was like a great gulf opening in front of him.

He stared back, speechlessly, and then he saw it.

Out of the corner of his eye he considered it and panic was gone. He was remembering, in every sharp detail, the red slashed signs across the polished glass that said the remodelled place would open on the seventeenth.

So there'd be no-one, would there, he asked himself, to wonder why the shop didn't open in the morning. And if anyone came and found no answer to their knocks they wouldn't worry. For one day. Would they? They'd think she'd been called away. And by the next day . . . by Tuesday . . . she'd be dead, wouldn't she? If she was locked in the vault that he could see from the corner of his eye, she would die. He wondered how much air there was in it, how long she would live . . . then wondering was swept away in the calm knowledge that he had found his way out. There was no need for a struggle, for the terrible face-to-face job of destroying her . . . there was need only for making her walk in.

He said, "Open the vault."

CHAPTER NINE

DEIDRE PENGHILL said brightly, too brightly, "These little things are sent to try us, I guess."

"My God!" In the middle of mopping his streaming face and head, her husband glared at her. "A flat in the middle of nowhere on a bloody awful stinker of a night and you say it's a little thing sent to try us! May the saints . . ." then abruptly, looking into her crumpled face, he started to laugh.

It was always the same, he thought ruefully. Deidre fluttered, she made impossible statements, she muddled the housekeeping, and burnt his breakfast toast, but she had only to look at him with her small olive-skinned face screwed up into what he privately called a hurt-monkey look, and he'd dissolve into laughter.

Big-boned, a little too heavy, he was still strikingly like Rachel—light brown hair, pale of face, and blue-eyed. Ann took after him. Secretly he was proud of it. Always he was glad of it. If Ann, too, had a screwed-up hurt-monkey expression whenever she stepped out of line, life would have been impossible from the discipline side of it.

He said grimly, "I'm as wet as a tadpole's backside. What's the time?"

She glanced at the small gold watch on her left wrist, then said laughingly, "Time for Linquist's Inquest, as Rachel calls it."

He grunted as she switched on the car radio. "Rae's a fool. Why doesn't she take up with some man who wants to settle down and marry?"

"Perhaps because she doesn't want to settle down and marry herself."

He set the car moving, listening idly to the music that came from the radio, till it finished and Stephen's quiet voice began to flow from the tiny set.

It was ten minutes later that the car was brought to an abrupt halt. He saw the look in Deidre's eyes, heard her panic-stricken voice and over it he said, "All right! All right!" and was conscious of shouting, of setting the car in motion again, of speeding down the wet dark road, with the windscreen wipers arcing an area of darkness ahead of him. "All right, I heard! It's over, don't you see that? It's over." His voice was calmer now. "Whoever was there has gone. Understand? And Ann's safe. Or he would have said so."

She only answered, "I've got to make sure. I've got to see for myself."

.   .   .

An almost delirious excitement had held him in its grip. He had gone back to the scooter, revved it into life and gone zooming through the town, out into the black, rain-swept night again, working out the release from panic that had swept him into an hysteria of relief.

Then as suddenly as it had happened it was gone. His whole body was tired, his hands shaking as they kept the scooter on the road. He almost idled his way back to the town, but he didn't, he knew, want to go back to Ivy. He couldn't. Not yet. Not while the exhaustion held, while his shaking hands could betray him to her searching gaze and questioning voice.

The thought of Spencers, of the gas-ring, of the jar of instant coffee with the torn label, of the chipped cups, was suddenly there in his mind and he knew that was where he was going. The key to the shop was on his key-ring. He had only to go in and light the gas and put on the battered kettle. It didn't matter that the coffee would have to be black. It would be better that way. And later, when his hands were steady and his mind clear again, he could safely go back to Ivy.

He came back to the street of shuttered shops from the

north, so that he didn't have to pass the shop by the lane, where the red slashed signs said, without knowledge of what was really to happen, "Opening on the 17th". He didn't so much as glance down the rain-swept street towards the place as he let himself into Spencers, standing there for a little in the darkness, with the hot musty smell of enclosed space about him, together with the smell of wrapping-paper and new clothing.

He went into the back part of the premises and pulled the dangling cord that switched on the unshaded bulb, revealing the tiny marble-chip sink and the rusty looking gas-ring. There was no lino on the floor of these back premises and his boots rang out hollowly on the boards as he moved about. He liked the sound, deliberately stamping to make it louder, because it was company for him. It didn't matter if anyone saw the light, even if the police came, because he was entitled to be there. Wasn't he? And it could never be connected with a woman stepping into her vault and letting the door swing shut behind her, locking her into death. Could it?

The more he thought of it, the way it was going to be put down to an accident, the more exultation swept over him, the feeling that fate had all along been sweeping along at full current on his behalf.

Deliberately he stamped his feet on the boards again, pouring boiling water into the brown powder in one of the chipped cups. Then, because he wanted more company than the sound of his own feet, he reached out a hand for the little transistor radio that was kept there for old Spencer's one vice in life. Switching it on he was thinking of the old man, five mornings a week, hunched over it, listening with pursed lips to the list of lottery numbers. The old man, to his certain knowledge, had never won anything in the whole time he had been there, but every day there was the ritual of listening to the prize numbers, and every afternoon the further ritual of stepping down to the tobacconist's to order another ticket.

The swell of music, church music he thought impatiently, seemed to fill the tiny space. Deliberately he turned it up further so that the crashing chords of it blotted out any thought at all.

He was still listening, washing up the used cup so that tomorrow there would be no trace of his being there, when the evening news session came on. The voice of Stephen Linquist was deep and quiet, attention-holding for all that, because of what he was saying.

He started to laugh, leaning there against the tiny sink, mirth bubbling in him. He wondered if Ivy was listening at home. She usually did. She had once described Stephen Linquist as a friend, telling a neighbour she felt he was that from listening to him night and morning for so long.

Then his laughter was gone. He was hearing the voice asking for anyone who had been by the lake that day to ring him. There was no reason given. There was none needed. He could feel coldness spreading through his body, the start of panic in the thought that after all Rose had been found far earlier than he had expected.

Then he told himself frantically that it didn't matter. Panic was lost in a sweet glow of relief, because the woman now wasn't listening, and reaching for the phone, and asking why she was wanted. And it didn't matter about the child. Did it? Because by now she would be asleep. She wouldn't hear it. And by the time she did . . . it would be too late then. Even if they went to the woman's place, and knocked — nothing would be done. They'd think she was away for a day, that was all. They couldn't possibly guess what had really happened to her.

Afterwards he felt how strange it was that relief was so slow to go; how he clung to it; reluctant to go on listening, to let reason tell him that something was wrong.

Because the deep quiet voice was warning — calling attention to girls who stood at bus stops with the one idea of getting an unknown date for an hour or two's thrill.

It was no coincidence. He told himself it couldn't be. But how had they known how it had happened? How had they guessed that Rose had stood at the bus stop and smiled at him when he had pulled up beside her, and gone quite willingly with him? How had they known that it had been a bus stop where she had stood and waited? Unless someone had seen them and told . . .

He left the unwiped cup and spoon there on the sink. The radio was still talking when he left the shop and went back to the scooter. He didn't even hear it. There was only one thought in him—to prove that after all it was a crazy coincidence. He had to get back home because if there was nothing wrong—if after all it was some frantic, crazy coincidence, Ivy would be there, placidly knitting, prepared to take him to task for getting wet and coming back late.

And if it wasn't a coincidence . . .

He parked the scooter two streets away and went padding softly towards the house, on the other side of the road. There was a dim light in the front room, and that was all wrong to start with, because they never sat in there unless there were visitors and then the lights were full on.

He turned sharply away and into the street at the back, moving silently up the side entrance of the house at the back of Ivy's, pushing his way through the thick hedge that grew between the two properties because there was no fence, crossing the narrow yardway silently. There was light spilling out from the kitchen windows, and in the glow of it he could see the fallen leaves from the flame tree, their red dulled by the night.

But because Rose was still, in spite of the news over the radio, a blur in his mind, it was difficult now to connect the leaves in the glowing light with the other leaves carpeting the ground by the lake.

He went across to the window and peered in. He could see Ivy. She was simply sitting there. Not knitting. Not reading. Just sitting and waiting, blank-faced, opposite a man in uniform.

. . .

For one minute Rachel had hoped it was Stephen—that after all, in spite of her telling him she wanted the coffee-pot and the place to herself, he had decided to come and join her. Because it was the first thing she thought of she delayed going down till she had slashed lipstick over her mouth and brushed her light brown hair to shining smoothness.

But she knew, running downstairs, the full skirts of her blue robe held high, that it wasn't Stephen, because of the urgency in the still ringing bell.

Standing still, her hands flat on the cold steel of the vault door, she felt only a wild outrage at what had happened afterwards. That she could have been such a fool rankled, but the thought of fire, of disaster, had simply swept away caution until it was too late.

He had been clever, she reflected in cool reasoning that tried to fight down the futile anger and resentment at her position. And he almost certainly didn't have a gun at all, only she hadn't dared to risk the consequences of challenging him, panicking him, perhaps proving herself wrong. You couldn't be certain of anything these days, she knew, and suddenly Stephen's voice was in her ears, speaking of young thugs, of senseless cruelty and bashings, of thefts.

Her anger started growing again, at the thought of the man prowling through the shop and upstairs, pawing through her things, perhaps beginning a ragging orgy of senseless destruction to pay her out for having nothing left around that was worth him stealing. Because the jewellery—the made-up silver and gold and the opals and semi-precious stones that were her stock, were all in the vault with her.

The thought almost made her laugh, it was a wonder, she reflected, that he hadn't thought of that before putting her inside. But once he had prowled through the place and found nothing he was going to open the vault again. Her mouth turned dry with panic at the thought as she wondered what he and she were going to do, face to face again.

She told herself that there was no point in heroics. Gun or not he could easily knock her out, badly hurt her, if she tried to fight him. And the stock was insured. Nothing, absolutely nothing, in the place was worth the risk of maiming or something worse happening to herself.

So when he came she decided, still standing there against the vault door, she would simply walk out and stand by while he did what he liked. She would fight down her rage, keep her mouth closed and her hands still. Afterwards there would be people who would say she had been spineless. It wouldn't matter. You had, she reflected, the dryness growing in her mouth, to be face to face with cold eyes and a white set face and to hear a shrill voice verging on murderous panic before you could know how you would act yourself.

And the police would surely know she had done the right thing. They must have seen the results of many cases where a woman, a man even, had played or tried to play the hero and paid for it. Stephen, too. He'd want to put her story into his session, want to interview her for everyone to listen to her first-hand account of what had happened. He'd want to . . .

And suddenly she was laughing, because the whole thing had taken on an air of the absurd. Stephen carefully making plain that women had no place in his life because that life was going to lead to places of danger. Stephen telling her how women needed a settled, ordered, safe existence — like her own. It all came welling back in memory. She wondered, still laughing, what he would say tomorrow about her calm, sane, ordered, safe existence. She leaned there, the laughter gone, picturing herself telling him what had happened, describing the man, mentioning the golden hair she had seen that afternoon by the lake — telling him how the man had worn a crash helmet when he had forced her into the vault, but she had still recognised the round features — telling him . . .

A slow shiver of fright went through her body. Describing him, she thought, and suddenly panic was with her, bringing cold sweat to her hands. Did he, the man now prowling through her premises, pawing through her things, perhaps smashing and destroying, realise that she could describe him to the police and have him put behind bars? Because if he did . . .

It was another reason why, when he opened the vault again, she had to be docile, pretend a quietness and not a raging anger at his behaviour. She had to let him take what he wanted and get out before he realised what a danger she was to him and did something . . . something it was beyond imagination to dwell on . . . about it.

She had no way of knowing the time. In the darkness of the vault it was impossible to see her wrist-watch and there was no light in the ceiling socket over her head. Timson had been going to bring a bulb for it in the morning when he came. Timson, she thought, and wondered if in the morning he would be able to fix the stairs or if the place would be so taken over by the police, so wrecked and damaged, that the job would have to be delayed yet again. It was ridiculous, considering everything else, how annoyed she felt over such a trifling point, but it was a relief to think of something else besides the man outside and the coming moment when they were going to be face to face again.

After a little she forgot Timson and began to wish the golden-haired man would hurry and come. The time seemed dragging endlessly. Surely there had been time and enough for him to ransack every cupboard in the small flat upstairs, for him to have smashed everything smashable . . . even, and left the whole place wrecked. And surely . . . didn't he want to get away for fear someone happened along? Wasn't he even one scrap afraid of being caught in the middle of his destructiveness?

The question grew and grew in her mind till it became a

thing of panic. Because if he wasn't frightened he was beyond common-sense—perhaps tightened up to what he was doing by drink or even drugs. If he was beyond fright or caring there was no knowing what he might do.

She wished he would come. She was sure that more than half an hour at least had passed since she had been inside in the enclosed darkness. She tried pressing her ear to the vault door in an effort to hear something from outside. There was nothing. And after a little, because she could no longer control her rising panic, she began to beat on the door and call.

. . .

Sandy said, "I never knew there was anyone who hated me that bad and what've I done anyway? Lloyd," her fingers, red-tipped, dug into the muscles of his thick arm. "What d'you reckon he would've done?"

"You want to have nightmares, you try reckoning it yourself," was the blunt retort. He eased her fingers off his arm with the other hand and shook her, gently. "Anyway what's to say he knew you from Eve? He could've just known there was a sitter and the sitter was a girl."

She said violently, "I'm never going to sit on my own any more and that's dead sure. Either I get you along or someone else . . ."

"You cut the idea out—about someone else."

She giggled, eyeing him from under suddenly lowered lashes. "I meant another girl, you big ape."

"You did?" His tone was gently jeering. "You wouldn't date with anyone but me, hmmm?"

"No." Her denial sounded absent-minded. "Lloyd, d'you reckon it was someone who was just playing a joke? Someone I'd turned down on a date who'd . . ."

"Well, if you like that idea better you stick with it," he told her generously. "I don't mind. Me, I'm not going to think about it. You're safe, aren't you?"

"Safe and scared silly."

"You might be more than scared silly if you were someone else?"

"And what's that mean?" She moved away from him to scrutinise herself in the driving mirror. They were still parked outside the Penghills' and with a jerk he set the car moving down the rain-washed, slippery road.

"I was just being clever. Thinking of what Linquist was saying. Didn't you hear him? I did while you were starting in phoning the Clancy woman. Talking about girls that cooked themselves a mess by standing around the streets waiting for a blind date."

She stared at him. "I'm still not with you."

"Well what'd he start spouting that line for? He was getting ready to spill a story, I bet. Only we never heard it all because of you finding out the Clancys never rung at all. And I saw Rose Gault today. All tarted up and waiting around in the street for something to happen."

She started to laugh. She said bluntly, "Rose's no little bud. You ought to know. You went round with her for a bit."

"So? Well I know her. But I didn't stop. But we live in the same street and there was a police car outside her place this afternoon. And later on I saw Linquist's car outside too. That was before you rang me. What do you reckon maybe you're not the only one got a fright today?"

Her eyes were round, frightened, then the fright gave way, slowly, to excitement. She said, "Do you mean maybe it was the same chap. That Rose got away from him and he tried it on me?"

"How should I know? I'm just putting two and two together and making forty-six to try and keep you from making ninety-eight out of your own imaginings about the bloke in the garage and now we're right back at you thinking of it again." He gave her a look of exasperation.

She didn't notice it. Patting a straying lock of hair into the tight little bun at the back of her head she said absently,

"Mum's been at me for ages to ask Rose how her dad was. He's in hospital. Only I never seemed to run into her. We could call in, couldn't we, on our way back?"

"At this hour?"

She flicked a glance at her wrist-watch. "Just past eleven. There's no harm in driving by and if they've lights on to stop off and make polite talk about her dad. And tell her about me and let her . . ."

"Curiosity killed the cat," was his mocking rejoinder.

She said grimly, "I keep thinking but for the cat *I* might've got killed."

.   .   .

It was the automatic movement of one hand towards the pocket of the full-skirted blue gown that reminded her, as her hand groped and caught at the comforting squareness of the cigarette case, that after all she did have a light, but her hands felt bruised and trembling from their pounding on the door, slow to flick the lighter flame into brightness.

And when she looked at the small face of the wrist-watch panic, instead of being defeated, grew closer, deadlier, like the stealthy approach of some jungle animal from the surrounding darkness.

She let the little light go out and leant against the door again, trying to beat back the darkness of mind and surroundings by closing her eyes, pretending childishly that she had only to open them and light would be there, if she needed it.

The trouble was it didn't work. She could still see, even with her eyes closed, the small black hands that told her that she had spent almost an hour in the close darkness of the vault. And an hour meant . . . what?

That he wasn't going to come back at all?

The thought was incredible, because if she held up the lighter and pulled the trays from the shelves she knew that the light would spark flame from the opals, and dull glowing light from gold and silver. She tried telling herself that of course he didn't know the trays were there, but common-sense reminded her that if he found no jewellery anywhere he must know for a certainty, even if he hadn't realised it before, that they would naturally be in the strong-room, under lock and key, with herself.

And yet he still hadn't come. It was quite unreasonable, when the premises were so small, when there were so few places to search.

She wondered, leaning there, if just outside, on the other side of the door, he was standing listening too, as panic-stricken as herself, wondering what to do—torn between greed at the idea of what the strong-room might hold and fear of what might happen if he re-opened the door. Was he afraid that there in the darkness she had found some weapon and was waiting to use it?

Because the thought that he might be hesitating for just that reason was unbearable, she beat again on the closed door and cried, even though she couldn't be sure that through the door he could hear her at all, "Open it. Please. Please, I can't hurt you."

Then later she stopped because she was afraid that her very insistence on the words might make him suspect she did indeed have a weapon and was trying to lull him into a false sense of security.

When she could no longer stand the darkness and silence and anticipation she flicked the lighter into flame again and could hardly believe that only another ten minutes had dragged by.

But even that, she thought impatiently, was an hour and ten minutes. Long enough for him to have searched the place twice over.

She forced herself then to look squarely at the crouching panic that had been waiting at the back of her mind, at the thought that perhaps he had been too afraid to re-open the vault and that he had gone away and left her. She told herself, even repeating the words aloud so that they echoed dully

UN–H

round her in the darkness, "It's not possible." Because he must have realised, surely, that a strong-room would have little or no ventilation, that locked in there she might easily suffocate if no-one came.

Panic came leaping full force then. The over-riding thought was suddenly of air—of how much or how little there was and would be. She walked slowly round the small space, holding her hands against the walls and floor, reaching up towards the ceiling, striving desperately to find some current of air.

It was, she realised soon, a useless exercise that brought her no conviction either way, but it brought to her a feeling of consolation, of surety that he would never have gone and left her locked up because he would have realised the danger of killing her.

Her groping hand in her pocket touched the lighter again and she fought down the temptation to light it once more, afraid of it burning up what little air there was. For the same reason she discounted the idea of a comforting cigarette.

She thrust both clenched trembling hands deep into the pockets of the blue gown, and then she knew that he had indeed gone away and she was trapped. Because when she had opened the vault she had had to take the keys from their drawer. She remembered how, putting the keys into the double locks, she had expected to be ordered to remove the trays of stones from their shelves and how shocked, how furious she had been at the shove in the middle of her back that had sent her sprawling to the vault's floor while the door slammed shut on her.

She remembered every detail of the whole thing—turning the keys, sliding them from the locks, making a half movement sideways, about to turn and face him, expecting, angrily waiting to be told to put her hands on to the trays of jewellery and bring them out to him.

And instead there had been the shove in her back.

And she remembered, her hands now clutched round the

114

keys in her pocket, how she had, making that small movement sideways, getting ready to go into the vault and remove the trays, she had slipped the keys from the locks and put them into the pocket of her gown. It was a gesture she used every time she opened the vault, because the door was self-locking when pressed shut and she had told herself one moment of forgetfulness and she might leave the keys in the lock one time, after closing it.

And now the keys were there with her in the vault. So no matter how much he wanted to get in, how frightened for her and of her he was, he could do nothing about it.

And the door didn't open from inside.

CHAPTER TEN

Rose had said sullenly, hand at throat, "I'm not allowed to talk about it, and it's not what you're thinking either. I knew him well enough. I thought him a real stick—him with his golden hair and his clean nails'n and fancy talk . . ."

That was what Sandy was thinking about as she and Lloyd got back into the car and he said, "Now you're here you'd best come to my place and have some coffee, then I'll take you home."

"I ought to be back now," Sandy pointed out with belated consideration. "I know Mrs. P. rang mum and told her not to panic if she'd heard about the prowler, but you don't know my mum when she gets the bit between her teeth—she's probably flat on the couch giving dad beans with a batch of hysterics."

Lloyd gave a jerk of laughter. "You make it sound like a dinner dish. Beans with a batch of hysterics," his deep voice went up to mimic her own.

She didn't appear to hear him. She said suddenly, "I've heard something about someone with golden hair. I wish I'd . . ."

He said in sudden anger, "In a minute you're going to say the bloke in the garage had golden hair, aren't you? You're just trying to scare yourself into fits and I'm not . . ."

"No, I'm not," her tone was injured. "I never saw anyone. I've said that already. It was something . . . it was Miss Penghill," she remembered abruptly. "Yes it was, Lloyd. Before I went. After she told me about Mrs. Swan she asked if I knew a man with golden hair. Yes, she did, Lloyd." Her eyes, bright with excitement, were turned to meet his scowl. "Now why'd she ask that? Do you think she saw someone hanging round the place and then . . . Lloyd!" her fingers were digging into his arm again, "Lloyd, I remember now. When that man rang—when he pretended to be Mrs. Clancy—he didn't think it was me. I remember now. He thought he was speaking to Mrs. Penghill. Not me at all. Mrs. Penghill. Lloyd, we'd better ring up and . . . ."

"No," his tone was hard, almost brutal. "No we're not. All we'd do ringing her is put the wind up her and Mr. Penghill and have the poor buggers starting at shadows all night long. And if someone—this bloke with the golden hair has been hanging around, Miss Penghill will give them the low-down in the morning. Won't she? Anyway if him and Rose's pick-up're the same, the cops are after him now. Aren't they? They might even have him by this time. So he can't do any harm. You and me," his tone was cajoling now, "are going to forget all about it and have an hour thinking about ourselves. Aren't we?"

．　　　　．　　　　．

It was after eleven by the time Agnes Swan had finished the phone-call she had been trying to make for most of the evening. By that time she was in her nightdress and grey dressing-gown, her greying dark hair in a bristling array of plastic rollers and when the call was finished she simply went on sitting there, unconscious of the chill of the room, her thin, chapped fingers pleating nervously at the tie belt of the gown.

Finally, the heelless mules flapping as she moved, she went into the front bedroom. Only the shaded light on her side of the bed was on, the shade tilted so that the light fell on the pale green wallpaper of the far wall, away from the hunched-up figure under the bedclothes. Her hand went out to the switch and the ceiling light glowed with brilliance. Over the sound of rising, angry protest from the pillow, Agnes said loudly, "Fred, there's something funny going on round here."

"Eh?" The bedclothes heaved and erupted the balding grey head of her husband. "Are you still harping . . ."

"All right, I know you think I've got in a fuss over nothing, but I still say that man sounded queer, and now there's something else I don't like and you're going to listen, so put your teeth in."

"For God's sake, why'd I need my teeth to *listen*?"

"Because I want you to talk it over." She reached impatiently for the glass on the bedside table, "Here! You know I can't bear you mumbling on without them. I got on to Miss Thatcher."

"What of it?" His voice was clearer, but no less impatient.

"You know what I wanted to ask her—whether any of the children had been talking about being rung up or their parents saying something on the same lines to Miss Thatcher or the teachers and I told her about Judy and everything and she said she hadn't heard of anything . . . and then, right out of the blue, she asked had Judy left a parcel somewhere in one of the shops. I thought for a tick she was fancying herself at calming me down and taking my mind off things, but I'll say one thing for her, she's not a fool and I said no, Judy hadn't or I'd have known about it surely and she said, 'Well it must have been Lynette then'. And the English child is Lynette and I said, 'Do you mean Lynette English?' and she said yes, because Lynette was the other one she'd named and the only one with brown pigtails."

She fell into frowning silence, her fingers reaching again for the tie belt, pleating in nervous desperation. After a minute he said quietly, "What are you in a state about over that?"

"Oh, I know I sound muddled, but there's . . . it's *nasty*, Fred—it's like some hunting creature quietly hunting down some defenceless baby animal . . ." she shook her head angrily. "I'm not telling this right. It was this way. When she said that, about Lynette and pigtails, I asked what she meant and she said that late this afternoon this man rang her up and said he was a store-keeper, only he never gave his name, Fred, and he rang off right in the middle of her asking, and that's odd to start with, isn't it? But he said some child had left a parcel in his store on Saturday and described the child—she was about nine, he thought, and had brown pigtails. And Miss Thatcher gave him Judy's name. And Lynette's, though she's older. She's so small she could be taken for a nine-year-old though. You know she is. And then he rang off.

"And Fred . . . don't you see? A man rang here and wanted to speak to Judy. He said he'd seen her, but just seeing her wouldn't give her name. And . . . if there wasn't something odd about it, why did he ring off, not try to explain who he was. And then . . . there was someone prowling round the English place tonight. Doesn't it sound like the same man, trying to find out where the child he'd seen lived, hunting her down . . ."

She was unconscious of the way her voice had risen to shrill panic. Even the touch of his big hand over hers, his quiet voice saying, "You're letting panic get away with you, Ag," didn't calm her. When he said, "There's nothing to say the man who rang Miss Thatcher wasn't exactly what he said. What would . . ." she broke in, as though she hadn't heard.

"It wasn't Lynette, if he was telling the truth. She's been at home all week with chicken-pox. Miss Thatcher forgot about that when she gave him Lynette's name. And it wasn't Judy. I never gave Judy any shopping to do on Saturday. She didn't have any parcels. But . . . Fred," her voice was suddenly steadier, as though panic had reached a peak and was forced to subside, "there was someone at the Penghill's tonight, too. And Ann Penghill is nine years old. And she has long brown hair. And for the last week, she's had it in plaits—aping Judy. Don't you see, Fred—he's looking for a child with long brown hair. It could be Judy, or Ann or . . ."

"Stop it!" he ordered loudly over her rising voice.

"But Fred . . ."

"I know. But he can't do anything. If it's Judy he saw she's

119

safe. And the Penghills will be on the alert tonight, too."

"I ought to ring them just the same. I ought to . . ."

"No! You get your dressing-gown off and hop into bed." His voice was firm against the panic of her objections. "What's the point in frightening the life out of them? They'll be on the alert already and this could be all a mistake. It could have been some innocent store-keeper right enough—for Pete's sake, Ag, Judy and Ann can't be the only kids in the district with long brown hair."

"Nine-year-olds," she reminded. "Nine-year-olds, he said. Miss Thatcher said she was going to ask at school in the morning if anyone had left a parcel anywhere."

"There you are then. You hop into bed, old girl. If there's anything in it the morning will show. Time enough to worry about it then. For now you hop into bed and forget it."

.   .   .

It was nearly midnight, the black hands on her watch showing plainly in the tiny flickering light of the cigarette-lighter, when Rachel gave up hope. Even when she had known that he couldn't let her out no matter what he did, there had been left the hope that he would realise she might die there in the darkness, and would get help.

She had told herself over and over again, fighting down rising panic with the calming thought that he had only to go to a call-box and disguise his voice while ringing the police and tell them what had happened and he would be safe and so would she, because the police when they came and saw the locked door would surely get in touch with Roger, as her brother, first thing, and Roger, as her solicitor as well, held a duplicate key to the vault.

And to her safety.

But then the reminder had come crashing back into thought that she had seen the man; had told him that she remembered seeing him before; that she could describe him and that he knew it. Even then she had fought desperately against falling into the final despair of thinking that he could have left her there deliberately in an effort to save his own skin.

She had puzzled dully over the fact that he had walked into the place with his face uncovered. Why had he done that, unless he had believed the showroom would be dimly lighted, that he would have time, once he was in and away from any prying eyes in the street, to pull a mask over his face. She wondered if that was how it had happened, if her sudden breaking into speech, warning him that she knew him, had startled him, thrown his plans aside and left him with one thing to do.

She had tried even then to convince herself that help would come because murder was a far different thing from theft. Only reason reminded that no-one would know it was murder. When she was found they'd think the door had some way closed of its own volition and trapped her.

Strangely enough it was that final thought that roused her from the dullness of witless fright. Anger came surging back, resentment that no-one would know the truth, determination that he wasn't going to get away with it.

The trouble was that neither anger, resentment nor determination gave her the means of getting free. She had to come down to that knowledge in the end, and to the fear, feeling sweat pricking gently on her skin under the blue robe's warmth, that soon the air in the vault would be used up.

But it had to last. She tried, groping in memory for things read and half digested in the past, to remember what one had to do in a place with little air. Wasn't there something about breathing shallowly? About staying still so as to use as little energy as possible?

What other steps could she take, she asked herself. Then the question was forgotten in the seizing on the one word— steps. Wild, sweet relief came flooding over her body and mind. Because in the morning Timson was due to fix the steps.

Her mind went skittering back over the interview the

previous Friday, hearing her own urgent voice saying, "I must have them fixed this week, Mr. Timson. I can't possibly have work going on once the shop opens and the steps are dangerous, especially near the bottom, so please . . ."

And he had promised, faithfully, definitely, that he would be there by eight o'clock on the Monday morning. Tomorrow. Eight o'clock tomorrow. So she had only to hold out till then and when he came she would knock and beat on the door and he must hear her. She was sure of it. And then he would get Roger.

She went on remembering her own voice telling him that on Monday she would be absent, that she was going to a jewellery exhibition in the city, driving both ways; to her saying that in case he was late she'd let him have the key of the shop door.

She pictured thankfully, blissfully, the handing over of the key as she had told herself it was quite safe because Timson was thoroughly reliable and anyway the vault would be locked.

But now she had only to hold out till eight o'clock and then he would be inside, close to the vault and he must, he had to, hear her beating on the door and calling.

And he'd get Roger. And after all she would be safe and free.

·   ·   ·

After the shock of seeing Ivy there, slack-bodied, empty-handed, just waiting, opposite the policeman, he had padded softly round to the front, where the dim light showed in the sitting-room. He had eased himself up on the balls of his feet and tried to look in through the tiny slit of open window at the bottom. He hadn't been able to see anything because the blinds were down, but he had smelt cigarette smoke and known there was someone there, too, in the half dark, waiting.

There had been only triumph in him when he had turned the scooter towards the north, bending over it, body hunched, sending it hurtling through the rain, knowing he had avoided the trap waiting for him. But gradually the triumph and exultation had died away, because he had realised he was riding into nothingness, into a future that was no future at all. The thoughts that had been with him in the coffee-shop, after he had left the lake, came clamouring back, reminding that wherever he went he needed money, a job, somewhere to live.

But there were houses to break into. Weren't there? Plenty of things to steal and to flog in some down at heel place where no questions were asked. He refused to think further ahead than the next few days, the next few weeks. The future after that would work itself out, someway, to his advantage. Wouldn't it? And anything, any drifting, any fighting, any stealing and scavenging was better, wasn't it, than turning the scooter and riding back into the trap that was waiting?

There was rage in him then at the way they had uncovered him after all. It was useless to wonder how it had happened like that, who had found Rose, who had seen them together and put the police on his track. All he could think of was the futility of all his planning, of his quiet stalking of the woman through the rain and night, of his shutting her in the vault.

He had no intention of going back, no compunction nor compassion at what he had done. The woman had stood in his way and now she didn't. If he went back and released her it wouldn't help him; it would only draw him further into a morass of trouble and might even lead to him being picked up by a prowling police car. And no-one, when she was finally found, could connect him with her. It would be put down to an accident on her own part.

Deliberately he turned his thoughts away from her, turning them into a blur hardly to be remembered, as he had done with Rose and all that had happened by the lake. All that was left

123

in him was rage at his being found out, at his having to run for safety, and the thought of the future.

When the scooter began to splutter and fail, he kicked at it impatiently, swearing, and then he realised what had happened —that the petrol had run out. He was forced to get off and push the little machine along the wet slippery road, panic coming back, his gaze continually going back over his shoulder, his eyes alert and afraid for signs of pursuit.

He nearly laughed when the service station suddenly loomed up on his left, because it seemed as though fate, even though sending him flying through the air, was still on his side, because in spite of the hour there was a self-service pump and he would be all right.

He pushed the scooter to the machine and fumbled for coins, realising with renewed fury that he was almost soaked to the skin and that ahead there were no dry clothes, no fire, no food waiting to comfort him.

His hands were shaking with cold and dampness as he slid the coins into the slot and reached for the hose and then, in the middle of filling the scooter's tank, he heard it, the shrill wail of a police car. He stood there, mouth gaping in sick panic, his whole body trembling, unconscious of the fact he had put too many coins into the pump's slot and that the petrol was spilling onto the ground. He just stood there while the beams of headlights swung on to him, caressed him briefly and darted on into the night and the sound grew less and less.

Then he started to laugh. Leaning there against the pump he laughed in an hysteria of relief. "You big boob," he almost yelled the words aloud into the night, "scared into a blue funk, you big boob!" and he spared time to wonder where the police car had been going, whether there had been a crash out there in the dark night, or a theft or something worse.

Because his body was still shaking in spite of the relief of laughter he groped in his pocket for cigarettes, pulled one from the packet with his gripping teeth and reached for matches.

He lit it, savouring the first lungful of smoke, tossing the match away.

Then he was staggering back, hands beating frantically at flames between him and the scooter, flames reaching out and catching him in orange light and searing heat.

CHAPTER ELEVEN

"So the silly bastard ran for it."

In the harsh light of the police room Giddings' face had a grey tinge, his eyes a red-rimmed ache for sleep. He pushed the phone impatiently aside and repeated, "So he ran for it and never went back home at all."

The constable the other side of the paper-strewn desk jerked, "The men at Deeford's place . . .?"

"They can come on in. Or wait, someone will have to break the news to the woman." He rubbed his hand irritably over his face, hearing the rasping sound of the palm meeting bristles. "He didn't only run for it—he landed himself in hospital. That was the police further north. Deeford was picked up in the road by a police car returning from a crash. He'd operated a self-service pump, foozled the job and completed the mess by tossing a match into some spilled petrol."

"Deliberately?"

"I doubt it. Would *you* take that sort of way out?" Giddings sounded astonished. "But maybe he can say what happened— maybe not. When they picked him up he wasn't capable of muttering anything except our Rose's name. Funny that, you know. Uppermost on his mind of course, but you'd think he'd be talking about the pain, wouldn't you? And the fire. But you can bet your sweet fanny no lawyer'd let us get away with talking in court of Deeford babbling in hospital of Rose Gault. The police up there thought he was muttering about a vault, actually. Fancied he might have done a smash job this way. They got his name out of the inside lid of the tool box on the scooter."

"You going out there, sir?" the constable suggested.

"No reason to. The docs have him knocked out for the present and if he comes round the men out there can take his statement. We'll see him when he can really talk and by then of course," his face mirrored his disgust, "he'll have had time to remember to keep his mouth shut." He yawned widely. "I'm off to bed. Tomorrow's another day."

"Full of prowler and pest complaints," was the constable's too cheerful rejoinder.

Giddings' reply, as he headed for the door, was curt, pithy and vulgar.

.   .   .

By three o'clock the sleep that had descended on her with astonishing suddenness had gone. Rachel was awake to the knowledge of stifling darkness, of a headache pounding furiously at her temples and a sickness that gripped at her stomach in cramping waves.

She had been lying flat on the floor, those half remembered notions of things read in the past telling her to do so, that that way she would conserve energy and air. Now she struggled to her feet and suddenly knew that she couldn't bear the warmth of the blue robe a moment longer. She unbuttoned it with sweating fingers, almost ripping it off her clammy body, leaving it huddled on the floor while she crouched there in a nylon slip, the cramps of stomach pain returning with renewed force.

It was then she reached in the pocket of the crumpled discarded robe for the lighter, flicking it into flame, reading the face of the watch, seeing in desperation and rising panic how the flame burned dully and low. It was a warning, with everything else—the rising warmth, the headache and stomach pains, that the air and her life were both running out. And it was still only three o'clock, which left five hours till Timson could possibly arrive.

She knew she wasn't going to make it; that she wouldn't be able to beat on the doors and draw his attention because long before he came the air would be finally gone.

She could feel the wetness of tears on her face and tried to rouse anger to stop them—anger at the futility of tears and anger at the man who had shut her in and at herself for having so tamely opened the vault in the first place. If she had fought him, refused to open it or get the keys he might have beaten her up, but it would have been better than the slow agony of dying in the vault.

Even sitting there the warmth seemed to be growing about her and for a suddenly startled moment she wondered, if he hadn't in some orgy of destruction, set the place on fire and what she was feeling in the vault was a reflection of heat from outside. It was so horrifying that she began to shake uncontrollably, rising to her feet, resting her body against the steel of the door, feeling even the steel warm instead of cold to her touch, now, beating on it with clenched hands, begging in hoarse, throat-straining cries to be let out.

It was the very hoarseness, the urgency of the sudden craving for something to drink that silenced her in the end because she had to think of something besides that searing thirst and think of it quickly. She began reasoning the situation out, telling herself that if the premises had been set on fire the flames would have burnt everything by this time—that the man had come four hours before. By now, if there had been fire, the place would be a charred mess and the fire brigade would have been there—she couldn't have failed, even in the silence of the vault, through her sleep, to hear the scream of fire-engines, of crashing beams and breaking walls from outside.

So there wasn't any fire.

And suddenly there was another memory in her mind—of the surveyor who had looked over the place for her. It was only a fleeting memory and she strove desperately to bring it into focus, knowing that it was something important, something that might help her to survive.

But it took a long time, while pain throbbed at her temples, while her stomach cramped and her throat burned, before she remembered being told that the vault wasn't fireproof.

And what else, her sluggish mind groped, had the wretched man said? There'd been a lot of it and she had paid little attention at the time because his plans for a new vault, a fireproof, completely burglar-proof . . .

That was it, she thought in sudden hope. He had told her the vault had never meant to be fireproof and burglar-proof. It had been put in by the tenants of twenty years before — at the end of the war when materials and workmen were scarce. She went on groping desperately, remembering the surveyor talking of those days, speaking of the way people had sought to protect precious papers and documents from thieves who broke in and maliciously tore up or burnt whatever they could reach in the way of papers.

But the vault had been a make-shift — its strong door to discourage any attempt to get in, its interior a shield against senseless destruction and nothing more. The surveyor had told her it wasn't fireproof or burglar-proof. She was back to that. He had urged her to get a proper vault put in and she had refused, because her stock of gold and silver was small, the opals and semi-precious stones she used not of vast value and the vault had seemed in its very bulk and impressiveness, a good enough safeguard till her finances were in better shape.

But why wasn't it burglar-proof? Her thoughts centred on that because if there was a way in for some desperate thief there must surely be a way out for her desperate self.

And then suddenly, completely, the memory was there. The side wall was simply the wall of the shop and it wasn't even a double wall, she remembered now. Between her and the wall of Wing Lee's café there was only a single cavity wall. The vault had used that wall as one side — the bricks being white-washed over and shelves put in. The surveyor, she remembered, had talked of someone breaking in through the wall from Wing Lee's and she had thought how absurd it sounded and how remote from fact.

But now . . . it didn't occur to her at once how absurd her idea of the wall collapsing at her bangings and letting her through, really was. She was scrabbling at the shelves, pulling out the jewellery trays, scattering them heedlessly to the floor with the crumpled blue gown. Then she had to toss them further while she groped again for the lighter. And when the little flame burned dully in her clammy hands, while her breath gasped and fought in her burning throat, she knew there was no way out still, because the shelves were steel and locked and bolted to the bricks.

She could feel the slow tears pricking at her eyes again and because of the futility of them, because she was determined not to break down, she fell to examining the wall with the tiny flame. Between the shelves the wall stood bare at the back of them, the whitewashed bricks a dirty grey in the feeble light.

She thought suddenly that if one of them was missing there would be a space—a space through which air might come. It was so swift an idea, so all embracing, that it swept everything else aside. Her hands went scrabbling fiercely over the bricks, feeling, gauging, trying to find some tiny crack in the mortar, some feeble trace of air, but there was nothing.

She was left finally in the darkness again, panting, trying to think clearly and swiftly, knowing that her life depended on her finding air.

She tried to think what the cavity wall would be like and was suddenly sure that if one of the bricks was out on her side air would flow from somewhere—up from the ground beneath the foundations probably or through some ventilator at the front of the buildings. But it would surely come from somewhere. And she had to get to it.

Her fingers went over the bricks closest to her, tracing the mortar, her teeth biting down hard into her lower lip as she fought down the tiredness, the sickness, that were urging her, above her desperation, to simply give up and sink down and sleep.

"I'm not going to," she said aloud and tried to think of something she could use on the mortar. She got to her feet again, fumbling through the trays still on the shelves, and then realised she had two weapons at least. When she had thought it was Stephen ringing her bell and had slashed lipstick across her mouth, she had slipped her feet into high-heel blue slippers. High heels—thin pointed heels with steel shanks. Steel shanks that could be used as a gouging tool on mortar.

She pulled one from her foot, closing her fingers over it and then, because it was more comfortable, because she could crouch forward and fight the cramps in her stomach when they came, because the air was better lower down, she crouched on the floor, gripping the shoe with the heel out-thrust, striking it towards the mortar on one of the bricks between the bottom shelves.

.   .   .

Agnes Swan rolled over in bed, switching on the lamp. She had been awake for a long time, listening to the quietness of the night now that the rain had stopped and the wind died down. It had been pleasant enough lying there in the warmth with her back against Fred's, but finally it had dawned on her that the back had a wakefulness about it, a rigidity that spoke of a determined effort not to move and disturb her, and she rolled over.

She said, "You're awake, Fred."

"Well what do you want me to do about it?" he asked sourly. "Get up and dance?"

"No. I was just lying here and thinking—over what that man said. He said he'd seen Judy and then he said something else, didn't he? About seeing her somewhere. In the reserve, wasn't it?"

"Dunno. What's the odds?"

"Just that Judy's never been down for weeks unless she's

been playing the fool, because I don't allow her down there not unless I'm there or someone else who's responsible because that lake's dangerous. You know how the women's club's been going on at the council about having the weeds cleared before summer. Well, I just don't allow her down there and unless she's been and never let on and I'll tan her if it's that because she's old enough to know I'm not going to allow that sort of caper, she hasn't been."

"Then maybe it wasn't the reserve."

"Maybe it wasn't Judy he saw," she responded, and the relief in her voice was plain. "It's like I said, before he's been looking for the kiddy he saw. He didn't know her name, but he could describe her and . . ." she broke off then said suddenly, "and it wasn't Lynette. I told you she's been home for a week. Why would he wait a week before he tried finding out who the kiddy was? She hasn't been anywhere because of the chicken-pox and . . ."

"You ought to go get a job with Inspector Maigret," he gave a choked snort of laughter under the bedclothes.

"Do you really think all this is funny?" she asked wonderingly. "Just a joke to . . ."

"No. But look, Ag, it's five in the morning and there's nought to be done about any of it. Have a talk to the police in the morning . . . this morning that is . . . if you'd feel better. But for Pete's sake go back to sleep."

He rolled over again, presenting his pyjama-striped back to her. She looked at it in silence for a moment, then reluctantly switched off the light. She said to the unresponsive back, "It was just I was wondering about little Ann Penghill. I'll get on to her mother . . ."

"In the morning. In the morning," was the mumbled response.

.   .   .

It was easier, yet harder, than she had hoped. Easier, because the mortar seemed soft and crumbling, almost eager to flake

132

away from round the brick, but much harder because the steel shank had no real point—the edge of it was the size of a threepence, and with that she had to gouge and pry. Harder, too, because of the cramping pains, the thundering pain at her temples and her gasping, sweating body that seemed to be wilfully disobeying her, so that when she struck hopefully, guiding the shank with her left hand, she struck at her hand and not at the mortar at all.

She hadn't dared use the help of the lighter flame, both because she feared it would run out and leave her helpless if she suddenly, desperately, needed light, and because she was afraid of the flame burning the air she needed herself.

But finally she had to pause—she had done that before but quickly she had recovered, and eagerness had urged her back to the job. But this time she lay flat, exhausted, her breast rising and falling in great terrible gulps that frightened her because of the remembrance that one should breathe shallowly in an airless place to conserve the precious oxygen. And she was gulping and fighting for it—using it up at an incredible rate, she was sure.

When she could pull herself upright she flicked the lighter on and nearly cried out because only three quarters of an hour had gone by and it had seemed like hours—long desperate frightened hours of urgency. She knew as she took up the blue slipper again that she had little time left. The air was growing increasingly bad and it wasn't just her imagination. Another hour of it seemed beyond bearing, yet she had to survive it and go on surviving until the brick came free.

Her shaking hands reached out and began working again, desperately.

She didn't know how long it was before finally the brick moved and her torn, bleeding, scratched fingers began tugging and pulling while her chest heaved in desperate gulps of frantic pain.

Then finally the brick came away—so suddenly, so easily,

133

that she toppled over and just lay there. Then slowly she dragged herself to the shelf, resting her face there and she could feel it — the musty, earth-smell of air coming from somewhere in the cavity wall.

Even in the midst of her gulping breaths she was laughing, unconscious of the extra pain it caused, only knowing that she had won and the man had lost; knowing that he was going to pay for all her pain and agony of the night; because now she could hold out till eight and at eight o'clock Timson would come, bringing Roger later, and then she would be safe.

•   •   •

Adelaide Timson shut her ears to the creak and her mind to the bumping, as she would close off the sound of hawking and blowing that would follow. It had been like that for the best part of the last fifteen years and it was the time of day she used now for thinking of the garden.

She thought of it, pursing her lips as she reflected on the night's storm, and the damage that would have resulted. Not, she reflected, that at the tail end of autumn there were her beloved roses to suffer, but the ground would be covered with leaves and débris and that meant the hated job of clearing up.

On the other side of the bed John Timson was beginning his day with the usual hawking and coughing and blowing that had started with a bout of bronchitis one winter and had continued ever since. Chesty, he thought glumly, like my dad and his mother before him. Chesty and none the better for the sort of weather they'd been having lately.

There was only one consolation in that sort of weather. Some of the sourness eased out of the wrinkles in his pointed face at the thought of pounds, shillings and pence. The night meant work and work meant cash and cash meant a little more of the house paid off and a little more off the station waggon and maybe a new washing-machine for Adelaide.

He said over his shoulder, "The phone should be ringing any minute."

Adelaide heaved herself upwards, a vast, billowing bolster of flesh that looked the larger for the shrunken wrinkled man the other side of the bed.

She said, "I clean forgot about that."

"No hurry. Let 'em wait." He spoke with the satisfied knowledge that they would wait all right and still be humbly thankful when the phone was finally answered and they could pour out their tales of damaged gutterings and broken roof tiles, cracked downpiping and torn-up trees. All the things that meant pounds, shillings and pence in his pockets because men who could put their hands to any job and do a good repair were worth speaking humbly to and waiting for.

Not that he overcharged or skimped a job, he thought complacently, reaching for his shirt and easing it over the thick wool of his underwear. He gave a fair day's work for decent pay and no-one could say fairer than that. Miss Penghill, now, had said that very thing to him . . .

He thought, Miss Penghill, and sucked in his shrunken lips and pushed them out again.

He said over his shoulder, "It won't be any use her worryin'. I just can't do it."

"What's that?" Adelaide was heaving her veined feet to the floor, sighing gustily as she set her full weight on their aged tenderness.

"I said she'll start in worryin' and it won't do a scrap of good. I'll have them finished right enough before Monday of next week. That's good enough, eh?"

"Maybe, if I knew what you were gabbling about."

"Miss Penghill," he looked at her in mild surprise. "I was talking about her and those stairs. Dangerous she says, and dangerous they are I quite agree. There was termites in that place one time. Told her so. Told her they'd rotted the boards of the stairs. Told her they should've been fixed time and time ago. And she had her heart set on me doing it today. But I can't. The phone'll be ringing any tick of the day now and it'll

135

keep on and it'll be 'My tree's come down' and 'my guttering's busted' and 'Timson, I've lost four tiles and I'm leaking fair and square on the eighty-guinea carpet'. A night like last, it's always the same. She ought to understand, eh?"

"Maybe, but she's not going to like it."

"I don't like catarrah, either, or rheumatics, but I got both. And I have to put up with 'em. And tomorra or Wednesday — there's no saying I mightn't get around to her by Wednesday. Friday say, at the outside. So I'll give her a ring . . . and there's the phone now." He sucked in his wrinkled mouth with satisfaction. "There's the first of 'em moaning and groaning and wantin' me at the double. I'll tend to it," he went shuffling out of the room, "and after I'll ring Miss Penghill and say I'm not coming. Got to be early because she's leaving early. So I'll ring . . ." his voice went muttering out of ear-shot towards the front of the house and the phone.

CHAPTER TWELVE

BREAKFAST was early because neither of them had slept, in spite of their having finally, after the fifth call seeking information, the fifth voice of excited friends seeking to revel in the sensation of the evening, taken the receiver off the hook and gone to bed. They had started to talk at dawn, too brightly, too determinedly of things that had nothing to do with the night.

And finally they had got up.

To Deidre there was further irritation in the fact that Ann was singing; had apparently spent the night in sleep after the wild confusion of their homecoming with Sandy almost in hysterics. Ann had drifted off in the middle of them still discussing with Sandy all that happened and Roger had carried the child to bed and apparently ever since Ann had slept dreamlessly. Deidre was annoyed simply because of the irritation towards the fact. It was quite unreasonable to feel that way and she knew it. She should, she told herself, putting water on to boil for eggs, be thoroughly thankful that Ann had been so little touched and alarmed by the night's events that she had gone so peacefully to sleep.

Instead there was the unreasoning irritation.

She looked up when Roger came into the kitchen, wearing just his pyjama pants, his face half shaven and the light brown hair, so like Ann's, disordered.

He said, "You know, I just thought, Rae probably tried getting hold of us last night."

"She'd have guessed we were fed up or tied up with the police or something and she wouldn't have worried. No-one was hurt. Anyway she could have gotten in touch with Stephen and had him tell her everything."

"I'd forgotten about that," he admitted. "I think though I'd maybe better call in on her this morning and tell her . . ."

"She won't be there," Deidre reminded. "She told me yesterday she was leaving at dawn for the city."

"Then she'll ring before she leaves. I'll go and put the phone back . . ."

"For God's sake no!" She stood there, her suddenly shaking hands thrust savagely into the drawer among the spoons and forks, without being conscious that the prongs of the latter were actually digging into her flesh.

Then she said, not turning, knowing that his face must look astonished, perhaps annoyed into the bargain, "I simply can't bear having that phone sitting there and having it ring and going and hearing some idiotic woman wanting to revel in the details and . . . try to scare me more by tales of Things That Happened To My Aunt Maude!" She essayed a laugh, heard it crack and break off and said flatly, "I've just had enough of it. And I don't want the phone to ring."

"I'm sorry. Then I'll call round on my way to the office. If Rae's there we'll have a natter. If she's gone . . . maybe she'll call in here on her way to town."

Deidre wasn't listening. She was saying, "Ann!" in a tone of exasperation, "for heaven's sake . . ." she shooed the child away from the stove. "Go and get your brush and let me fix your hair. You look like an hysterical mermaid with it whirling around you that way."

Ann giggled. She said, holding out the brush, "Mummy, last night . . ."

The brush yanked savagely at the soft brown hair. "I've heard enough about last night! Do you understand? We're not," she fought and found a tone of sweet reasonableness that contrasted completely with the boiling turmoil inside her thoughts, "we're not going to speak of it any more. Ever.

It's all in the past and we're not going to talk to people about it any more."

"I was only saying that Mr. Linquist . . ."

"No! No, we're not even going to talk to reporters either, Ann. Understand? Not even Mr. Linquist. Because he's a reporter first and a friend of ours last and we don't want any more publicity." She spoke each word clearly, stressing them, trying to impress them on the child's mind.

"The police . . ." the small voice was uncertain.

"We don't want anything more to do with the police either. We've had enough publicity and fuss. That's all I want to hear about it, Ann. Understand? Now," her voice was falsely bright, "let's talk about something else. Let's talk about school. And your hair. Are you going to have plaits today?"

.   .   .

Stephen Linquist woke early to the clouded-skyed day that had dawned after the rain, but he made no effort to start showering and dressing. Instead he reached out to the bedside table for cigarettes and matches and lay there, one arm behind his dark head, smoking, summing up the day ahead, wondering how much copy, how much sense and how many lies it held for him.

There was Rose for a start.

He grimaced at the thought of her. Now with the night behind her and freedom from having to stay quiet given to her, she would have a bigger and better story ready for anyone who would listen. She would be preparing to revel in the publicity and everything she was going to say from now on would be angled to put herself in the best possible light.

He decided that so far as he himself was concerned she was going to be disappointed. He wasn't going to go near her.

His first job of the day was going to get hold of all that Giddings would allow him and then there would be interviews with the man's family, his friends and employers—a vast number of interviews, thousands of words, out of which he would draw perhaps a couple of hundred to sketch to his listeners the character of the man who had picked up Rose and then nearly killed her.

He lay back, turning over the night's alarms in his thoughts. He didn't think there was anything more for him in the prowler stories. He didn't know whether he believed Sandy Micklin's tale or not and he didn't much care. It was something that would be quickly swallowed up in the more exciting news about Rose.

He didn't see that anyone involved in the prowler scares could give him anything more. Helga English had proved a quiet, controlled woman the previous evening. Not the sort to want any more publicity, to embroider her story or give him more than a cool "No comment" if he called again.

Agnes Swan was a different proposition, but he didn't know that he wanted anything more from her either. She wasn't the Rose type who would deliberately embroider, but time and continued dwelling on her panic would make her unwittingly add to the story till it bore little relation to the truth.

Watching the little stream of smoke rise from his cigarette towards the ceiling of the room, he dismissed the subject from his mind.

He thought then of Rachel.

He wanted to see her again and he didn't. He wanted to sit opposite her and watch her face break into the wide-mouthed smile that was her chief beauty; he wanted to listen to her deep voice and watch the way her eyes changed colour in different lights, in small turnings of her head, from blue to grey.

And he didn't want to go near her because there could be nothing better between them than their present friendship; the coming goodbye. It had to be that way because his work held no place for a woman.

He knew and knew too that it was a sign of weakness in his character that he was going to call in and see her that morning just the same.

As he pulled out of bed and padded to the shower he knew what excuses he was going to make for the call. He'd discuss the previous night; ask her what she thought of Sandy's story. It didn't matter that he had already decided the prowler stories held no meat for him. He'd ask Rachel's opinion and listen to her deep voice and decide all over again that it was simply no good — that he wasn't going to ask her to marry him because his work was going to spell danger in the future and he wasn't going to drag her into that.

But when he reached Provence Street and pulled up and stepped out of the car on to the grey footpath, he stood frowning. The blinds in the flat upstairs were still drawn and the windows were blank-faced. And a full milk bottle was still on the front step.

He debated the idea of waking her, glancing at his watch, seeing it was just short still of a quarter to eight. If he woke her she'd invite him to breakfast; there'd be time to talk.

But he wasn't going to talk. He wasn't going to sit opposite her, watching her as she sat there in dressing-gown and slippers, her face still sleep-flushed, knowing that he could have her like that every morning of his life if he wanted to speak out.

He went back to the car and started it, driving away without looking back.

. . .

When she woke again it was with the mustiness of dirt and earth and stale air in her mouth and nostrils, a clammy stickness on her body and the ever increasing desire for water burning deep in her throat.

When she flicked on the lighter again the little flame burned brighter, but still, she was certain, not as brightly as normally. Her still throbbing temples and the continued cramps in chest and stomach told her the air was by no means good. But the little light showed her it was half past seven.

She pulled herself slowly into a sitting position, and suddenly, ridiculously, so ridiculously that her stiff, cracked lips curved into laughter, she was worrying about her appearance, wondering what she would look like when Timson and Roger opened the vault; wondering if perhaps there would be other people standing there to see her and if she would look terrible, with her hair disordered, her lips cracked, her face sweat-streaked.

In sudden modesty she pulled the robe from the floor of the vault, shaking it out, exclaiming to herself over the creases in it and finally slipping her arms into it and buttoning it down the front. Then she felt through the scattered jumble on the floor, selecting finally a light wooden tray, carelessly scattering the silver brooches from it in a heedless jumble on the floor.

She tried it, banging it ruthlessly against the door of the vault. The noise surprised her. It seemed to echo thunderously around her. Then surprise gave way to delight. Because she was certain, trying it again in almost delirious relief, that Timson would hear it at once.

She tried to imagine what he would do at first. He would probably waste time in trying to open the vault or find the keys. Then he would get Roger. And afterwards . . .

It wasn't going to be pleasant, facing the police and later going to court when the man was arrested. She hoped, in anger, that he would definitely be caught. She hoped too that he didn't get a lenient jury, a lenient judge. She considered it a pity that by the time the case came courtwards her hands would be healed, so she couldn't thrust them under the eyes of a jury to show them how she had scratched and torn over finding air for herself in the locked vault. She felt that it was an injustice that men who had never been locked in a place like this, never experienced the terror, the aching agony, the fight for air, should try a man who had shut her in. Perhaps they would discount half her story, and put it down to hysteria. And a good lawyer — some friend of Roger's probably, someone she knew—would try to minimise the thing so that his client would get off lightly.

And the injustice of it wouldn't finish with that either. There would be all the irritation and unpleasant publicity of reporters to face. There would be Stephen to face . . .

The humour that had come to her hours before came sweeping back. Stephen was going to be confounded. She wondered what words he would find to describe her present situation.

Then abruptly conjecture was gone. Frantically she flicked the lighter into flame again, realising she had completely forgotten that time was passing. But it was still over ten minutes till eight o'clock—before Timson was due.

But she decided all the same not to delay. He might possibly be early. She had told him she was leaving by eight-fifteen at the outside. That was why she had given him the key to the place, in case he was delayed twenty minutes or so in his coming.

She picked up the tray and knocked it slowly, heavily, against the door of the vault, swinging her arm and wrist in what was soon an automatic movement.

•   •   •

It wasn't what he called a breakfast at all, Timson decided, scowling down at the last piece of blackened toast. Enough was enough and too much of a good thing was as maddening as too much of a bad.

He had expected phone-calls in plenty but not all that had come; not the one coming after the other so that Adelaide had been kept busy plodding from kitchen to phone, and never getting down to what he called proper cooking.

And in the end she said firmly, "It's no good me botherin', that's all. You can make do with toast and a big pot of tea and then you'd better be off. The way it's going Miss Penghill'll be lucky to see you Friday week." There had been a speculative gleam; an anticipatory pleasure in her thoughtful, "There's a ten per cent discount this month on washing-machines."

She went plodding away to answer the phone's shrill summons yet again, not giving him chance enough to retort there was ninety per cent chance of him getting pneumonia or something worse from lack of proper food before the day was over. There was still a chill in his thin body in spite of the hot tea as he muttered and grumbled his way out to the station waggon, checked that his tools were in and the ladder roped to the top and eased himself into the seat. He could hear the phone still ringing as he took the waggon out into the road and swung towards Provence Street and the shopping centre.

With the ringing there'd been no chance to call Miss Penghill. Not that it mattered, he had decided. It was better to get off and away before Adelaide stood promising any more people he'd be there "right-off". Now that he was gone she would have to say his day's list was full and he'd come in the morrow instead.

He would, he decided, scrawl a note to Miss Penghill and slip it under the door. That was better even than ringing her and having to start arguing. Women always argued. Even if it was only the set of a bathroom tap they wanted an argument about it. He had no patience with it. And no time for one that morning with half the town in trouble.

He pulled up short of the shopping centre and found a stub of pencil in his pocket. On a leaf torn from a pocket diary he scrawled, "Dear Miss Penghill, can't come. Too many leaks from rain. Be down Wednesday possibly, Thursday or Friday certain. Yours to oblige, J. Timson," regarded it with satisfaction and left the station waggon to walk across the road to the shop.

There was a car just pulling away from the front of it. He recognised the car and the driver and he wondered, opening the turnip watch that he still carried in spite of Adelaide always nagging him to get a wrist one, why Stephen Linquist was calling on the girl at seven-forty-five in the morning.

Then he nodded slowly. The business of the previous night

of course. A prowler at the Penghills'. All a lot of nonsense in his opinion. In Adelaide's too. The pair of them had talked it over and nodded their heads and agreed the youngsters of today weren't a patch on yesterday's. Give the present lot a story about prowlers and they started yelling their heads off and trembling at shadows, and wanting themselves in the papers with a line under their photos saying they were dishing up bacon and eggs come the day they took up modelling.

He'd model them, he had told Adelaide. Model their rears with the back of a hairbrush, that's what he'd do. They didn't seem to think their elders didn't want a lot of publicicity. The Penghills now. Like as not they were wild as hornets this morning.

Which was why, he decided, reaching the shop, Stephen Linquist had come prowling round so early. Like as not the solicitor and his wife had told Linquist to chase himself. So he'd wanted a story from Miss Penghill. But he hadn't got out because the milk was on the step and evidently he'd got no answer to his ringing, so Miss Penghill must have already gone.

He stopped, grunting, to slip his note through the post slit in the doorway and turned away, then hesitated. His gaze went to the milk bottle and he reached in his pocket, withdrawing the key. He might as well, he reflected go on up and put the milk in the refrigerator for her. If it was left that way all day the sun would sour it for a certainty.

The key was hard to turn and he cursed, opening the door at last and slipping upstairs, nodding to himself, muttering, "Dangerous enough" as he trod on the lower ones.

When he got to the top he stood blinking, surprised, suddenly embarrassed, because the lights were on in the sitting-room, and the blinds were still drawn. He cleared his throat, rumbled "Miss Penghill" into the silence and pursed his lips.

Now that was funny, wasn't it, he reflected. Light on, curtains drawn and milk on the step. And the bed not slept in.

He peered into the tiny bedroom and raised his eyebrows in astonishment, then shook his head. No, she'd slept there and made it up again neat and tidy that morning of course and then she'd left in a tearing hurry. And forgotten the lamp of course.

He scratched his head. It was funny though, wasn't it. Remembering to make the bed all neat and tidy, but forgetting the curtains and the light. And the milk.

Lord, he thought in amazement, she couldn't have left before the milk came. That came round at five in the morning. She hadn't left in the dark. That would have been mad.

Remembrance of the night's events popped into his thoughts. Prowlers, he thought and suddenly there was alarm in his face, that gave way to amusement.

"You're an old fool," he told his reflection in the dressing-table mirror. " 'Course she never slept here last night. That sister-in-law of hers was all of a twitter, I'll bet anything. Rung her up and asked her to come and hold her hand all night. And off she went in a hurry, and forgot her light. That's it."

Then he scowled, looking at the milk in his hand. He'd better be off himself in a hurry. That was what. Ten to one she'd look in at the shop on her way to the city. She might need other clothes. All sorts of things. And if she found him there there was going to be a scene. He shuddered. She'd argue and fuss and remind him he'd promised about the stairs.

Hurriedly he put the milk away and went down again. By the time he had closed the shop door and gone back towards the waggon he had forgotten her in thoughts of the work that lay ahead.

CHAPTER THIRTEEN

GIDDINGS sat in the pale glow of sunlight stretching out through thinning cloud, but there was no brightness in his expression as he gave the other man the briefest of details. There had been a brief paragraph in the morning papers mentioning the tragedy on the northern highway, but there had been no connection made between the injured man and Rose's story.

He said, turning deliberately away from the younger man, "That's all I have to say, so . . ."

"It's a funny thing," Stephen might not have heard the heavy hint or the impatient rustling of papers in the other's hands, "that he was still so close to town when he was hurt. It was hours since he'd dealt with Rose. What was he doing in the interval?"

Giddings scowled. "Hanging around town somewhere. Making an alibi for himself maybe. I wouldn't know and I don't care. It hardly matters." He went on impatiently, after a moment's silence, "He meant to go home. He went if I'm right. Someone got through the hedge between the Deeford place and the place at the back. You can see where, and there's bits of hedge, where they might've stuck to wet clothes, then been flicked off by the wind, all along the path up to the kitchen windows. He came in by the back and had a look-see, saw my man and lit out." He added a brief satisfaction, "Let some smart lawyer try laughing that point off. A man without a guilty conscience doesn't come sneaking home through a hedge and go for his life on seeing a policeman sitting with his sis in the kitchen. For all he could tell they might be courting!" He gave a rumble of laughter.

Stephen was thinking of Martin Deeford's secret return to the house when he first saw Ivy. The compassion that was always there in spite of years of interviews, was wondering how she had felt through the ordeal of waiting with the policeman opposite her and her brother somewhere outside in the storm. But Ivy Deeford seemed to have no need for compassion. He was repelled by her chill courtesy, her flat-voiced statements that seemed to hide nothing at all from the shame of future publicity. Perhaps, he thought after leaving her, he should have congratulated her on the common-sense that might have been at the back of her attitude, telling her that however much she might twist and turn every last thing about her brother and herself was going to come to light. He still found her repelling though.

He had pulled up at the garage, given his order for petrol and was fumbling for his note-case before he realised the young giant handling the pump was Lloyd Thompson.

He said harshly, looking at the dark head bent over the car and pump hose, "How much of that story of yours and Sandy's was true?"

The hose jerked and he was looking into the oil-bright darkness of the youngster's eyes.

The big shoulders moved in a brief shrug. "Sandy guessed a lot of folk'd take a chance to run us down. You can think what you like, mister."

Stephen eyed the hard face thoughtfully. He said at last, "You're not a scrap worried. Why aren't you? She's your girl. Why aren't you frightened the man might have another shot at her . . . if the story's true."

The dark eyes narrowed slightly, then Lloyd unhooked the hose from the car, screwed the petrol cap back and said, "That's not bad. You seeing that. The story was true. So far as I know. I wasn't there. Get it? I wasn't around. She didn't ring me till after. And I was scared for her all right. And now I'm not. O.K. But now I know it wasn't personal. You get that? It wasn't Sandy he had it in for, on the personal side. Did you know that about that woman ringing and asking Sandy to go chase a dog wasn't true? After she and me chased a dog and rang the woman and said come chase it yourself, the woman said she hadn't rung. So it was someone lured Sandy out deliberate. I felt sick right down in my belly. Then later on she remembered something—the man who'd rung called her Mrs. Penghill and gave her no time to say she wasn't. So it wasn't personal. Not for Sandy."

"Have you told Mrs. Penghill this?"

"No. Should we or shouldn't we? I don't just know. Mrs. Penghill I'd guess is like old Duckfeathers." He grinned without any laughter in his eyes. "Mrs. Swan to you, mister. They get in a flap easy I'd say. I wouldn't say it was personal to Mrs. Penghill either, it was just the bloke thought her alone in the house because the car was out, see, and he could tell that—the garage doors were wide open. He must've thought Mr. Penghill was out and his wife was a sitting duck."

"The same as at the English house? The man of the place was away there, too."

"She wasn't rung up," Lloyd reminded.

"No phone on," Stephen gave back crisply. "But there was a crash—an effort to bring her out investigating would you say?"

"Maybe."

When the petrol was paid for and Stephen was sliding behind the wheel Lloyd asked, "You going to tell the Penghills?"

"I'm like you, should we or shouldn't we?" Stephen confided. "Maybe I'll see Mr. Penghill."

So the story was true he thought as he drove away. Sandy wouldn't have bothered embroidering to Lloyd alone; if they'd made the whole thing up they would have told the further embroidery to the Penghills. And it was true that there had been a man in the night seeking houses where the man of the place was away and the woman could be lured outside. Not a pretty thought. But women alone ran that risk any night and knew it and now for weeks ahead any woman on her own would keep inside. That was certain.

As for Mrs. Swan — he grinned, remembering Lloyd and Old Duckfeathers — that was a different thing again. One man after a child. Another after women on their own. And yet another fleeing through the darkness after assaulting a girl. What an unquiet Sunday night it had been.

He thought suddenly that he would tell Rachel of Lloyd's story. She could tell it to Roger or not, as she decided herself and Roger could take what action he pleased.

But there was no reply to his ringing at the shop door, though the milk bottle had gone from the step. It was then he remembered her saying, some days before, that she was going to a jewellery exhibition in the city.

Impatiently, throwing away a just-lit cigarette, he turned his back on the shuttered shop and went back to the car.

It wasn't till he was about to slide into the driving-seat that he noticed the dog. It slunk, belly close to the ground, from the lane beside Rachel's shop, its brown eyes hopeful, tail slowly wagging.

He said "Hello boy" and the dog jumped, bounded towards him in pathetic eagerness, tail vibrating hopefully, the whole thin body expectant.

He frowned, bending to pat the rough-coated head. "What is it? Did she forget you this morning?" It wasn't he reflected, still frowning, like Rachel to have forgotten the creature. She had found it, a starving, snarling stray, living in the back of her premises when she had moved in and with her adoption of it it had grown to docility and a certain rib-covered sleekness of body. She had, he remembered, asked his advice about medicines for the brute, with an absorption that had touched and faintly irritated him, because it had seemed such a waste of maternal instinct. He had wanted to snap at her, "Find yourself a husband and have half a dozen children, Rachel," and had stopped himself from the cruelty only because the thought of her as someone else's wife had been almost unbearable, even though he had told himself it was what he wanted—her safely married to someone else so he could forget her.

And now she had forgotten the dog. He looked frowningly upwards to where the blinds were still closely drawn and abruptly he moved into the lane, the dog bounding expectantly at his side.

He went into the tiny area at the back of the shop, through the small gateway from the lane. He could see the dog's water dish, under cover from the rain, was dry now and the other dish was empty and had obviously held no food that morning.

In sudden anxiety he wondered if something was wrong; if she was ill, then he remembered the milk had been removed from the step and that before there had been a light showing in the curtained window facing Provence Street. That was out now. He suddenly laughed. He said, bending to pat the dog again, "Know what? Your lazy mistress slept in this morning and she had to run, without her own breakfast for a certainty, and forgetting yours, too. She even forgot to pull back the curtains. All right then, boy, I'll get your breakfast and we'll both snap at her when we see her next, eh?"

· · ·

For once Hilda Thatcher's wide, professional bright smile was missing. She had been looking out the window at a squad of the children drilling in a half-hearted manner under the urging of a girl little older than themselves and thinking·in irritation that her new support was far from that; that she was a scared homesick child and not a teacher at all, when the knock came on the door.

She said, "Come in" and turned to nod to the grey-haired, thin-lipped woman who came hesitantly in.

"Good morning, Miss Tiens." Then she smiled, sketching a little gesture of impatience. "That's the fourth time I've said that to you this morning. But . . . my mind's clogged."

"Why?" the elder woman sat down without being asked.

Hilda Thatcher gazed at her with faint irritation and sighed. Miss Tiens was a trial. She was old and she didn't really like children and these days her mind was on her coming retirement and pension, but at that she was still a lot better than the child taking the drill squad outside.

Then impatiently she shrugged away the thought of the problems that Miss Tien's retirement was going to pose and answered the older woman's curt question with an equally curt, "This prowler affair."

"Why? Hasn't been anybody prowling around these premises. It isn't our business."

"He's been prowling round the children seemingly and that definitely is. I've had Judith Swan's mother on the phone."

"A stupid woman," the statement was given without anger or irritation, merely as an addition to the headmistress's own comment.

"Perhaps, but not where Judith's concerned. It's a strange thing, you know, but where a woman's children are the cause of . . ." she suddenly frowned, "but never mind that. What I wanted to say is, Mrs. Swan thinks this prowler saw one of the children in the reserve in the past few days and has been trying to find out who she is. I think I agree. You heard me ask at assembly for some girl who left a parcel in one of the stores? None of them came forward. They didn't know what I was talking about."

She went on, choosing her words with care, speaking of the man who had rung her the previous day and been given the names of Judith and Lynette English.

"If it's a coincidence, it's an unfortunate one," she said bluntly. "Judith was rung up, Lynette's house had someone prowling around and so did the Penghill house. And Ann Penghill has long hair. Long brown hair. Also, she's nine years old."

"You're not responsible for the child," was the cold reminder.

In rising irritation, looking into the pale, unblinking gaze turned towards her, the younger woman said, "You can't turn away from things like this because it can't strictly be called our problem. You took Ann's class and the ten-year-olds, to the reserve on Wednesday for a botany lesson. What I want to know is . . ."

The answer came with scornful impatience. "If I'd seen something wrong, any man prowling about, I'd have said. Long ago."

"Well . . . of course I expected you to say that, but he wouldn't have stuck himself out in full view like a sore thumb. I told Mrs. Swan about Wednesday's outing and that it needn't be Ann or Judith he saw. Pauline has long hair. I'd call it darkish blonde. A man might call it light brown if he saw her only in shadow.

"But that isn't the point. I've promised Mrs. Swan that from now on a watch will be kept, as the girls leave. From your room you can see right round the school. If there's anyone—if a man appears and follows one of the girls . . ."

Miss Tiens stood up. She said, "You won't mention this to the children of course. It will simply give them a chance to invent things. But what about the parents?"

"I thought I'd bring the subject up at the parents' meeting on Thursday. After last night's publicity the man will be scared away I should think. Don't you? So there's no hurry. Is there?"

. . .

She had been forced to pause for long periods at a time, when her body had simply refused to obey her commands and her arm had lain uselessly at her side, though her brain had urged and begged the fingers to reach out and pick up the tray and bang again and again at the door.

With each pause she had resolutely refused to flick the

153

lighter into flame again and look at her watch, telling herself with grim determination that very little time had passed; that Timson was only a little late and would be there any moment.

But finally she gave in and when the lighter was burning above her left wrist she cried out, in a panic that was a searing pain as bad as the throbbing at her temples. Because it was half past ten. And Timson hadn't come. She was certain of that, because he couldn't, she was sure, have failed to hear the banging, from the vault, and done something about it. Even if he had gone for Roger and been delayed in finding him he would have, before leaving, knocked back on the vault, encouraging her, telling her by his knocking that she had been heard and was getting help.

No-one, she had told herself, would be so stupid as not to do exactly that. All along she had given five knocks and stopped to listen, expecting each time to hear a knock in reply and to know he was there the other side of the vault's door.

But now it was half past ten and nothing at all had happened.

She crouched there, shaken and sick and furiously angry. That he had broken his promise was unbearable.

"I'll never employ him again," she cried aloud and the words echoed dully round the vault, mocking her, reminding her in sudden terrible clarity that if someone didn't come soon she wouldn't be capable of employing anyone, ever.

The thirst that had been there, a burning pain, at the back of her mind all the time she had knocked on the door, was back and worse than ever, making breathing more difficult than ever. She wondered how long she would be able to last before the pain of it, the burning desire, turned her into a crazy, unreasoning creature battering bruised hands uselessly on a door that refused to open.

The picture looming there in her mind was so frightening that she started to shake, started to grope frantically for the tray with the now dented corner, started to close her fingers round it.

And then she knew she had to sleep. The knowledge came with devastating suddenness, overwhelming every other feeling. She tried to fight against it and then, because the thought came that sleep would blot out the burning desire for water, she simply let herself relax and there was only darkness, that just as suddenly as it had come, dissolved again in the panic of consciousness, in a scrabble for the lighter, for the flicking on of the flame and the seeing that she had been asleep for over half an hour.

The air seemed to smell much mustier. In an effort to clear her brain, to revive her, she pressed her face down to the bottom shelf, towards the open space where the brick had been.

And she saw it. Just a flicker and then it was gone. But she screamed. And went on screaming, unable to stop, and revelling suddenly in the sound because it meant that the creature — the huge rat that had been watching her through the opening — would be running from it through the cavity, down into the foundations of the building, into some hole out of her sight.

Something the surveyor had told her seared back into her thoughts. He had said there were rats in the place, that it was only to be expected in a group of buildings as old as the group of which hers was one. He had urged her to speak to the other tenants in the block, to make a concerted effort to stamp them out. She had baulked at it. On the score of expense again. It had been something, along with the idea of a new vault, that she had pigeon-holed in her mind for some time in the future.

She wondered how many of them there might be running endlessly through the group of buildings, then resolutely closed her mind down on the thought. The sudden silence had brought it to the hole of course, to peer into the vault. Probably the whole colony of the horrors had been listening to her bangings and callings and when it had ceased one of them . . .

Firmly she pushed the thought aside, deliberately, because she had to have air, she put her face down to the bottom shelf, breathing deeply of what air there was. Then she began banging again. She didn't know what time it was when she stopped, but it had seemed a terrible age of time. She refused to turn on the lighter because the passing of time was something she felt she was better off not knowing about.

She sat there getting back her strength for another attempt, speculating on what was going on outside, forcing her mind to dwell on the street beyond, wondering if it was sunshine or rain out there.

Sunshine or rain . . .

She suddenly knew why Timson hadn't come and slow tears of rebellion welled in her eyes. She started upbraiding herself uselessly for not realising that the storm would have brought havoc all through the town and that Timson would have put her repairs at the bottom of his list. He wouldn't come that day. He mightn't come the next either. Or the next . . .

Panic came leaping back and she tried to fight it by forcing herself to think slowly and clearly of the days ahead, picturing people who might come, people who would wonder where she was.

She thought of Roger and Deidre and slowly hope in them eased out of her mind and was gone. Roger and Deidre knew she was busy with last minute details ready for the next week's opening. If she didn't come near them; if she didn't ring or call, they wouldn't wonder and they wouldn't break in on what they considered her privacy. She remembered how apologetic Deidre had been the previous day over asking her to take Ann for the day. They wouldn't be likely, unless some terrible emergency happened, to call on her for anything for the rest of the week. They would feel that after Sunday they had already imposed too much.

Which left Stephen. And she knew he wouldn't come either. She had rebuffed him the previous evening. He was probably glad of it. If she didn't answer his phone-calls he would think it was deliberate, that she didn't want to see him again before he left. He would be glad of that, too. The thought of it was unbearable.

And that left—who out of all the world would worry about her?

There was Timson, who mightn't come till the week-end. There were the people she had meant to see at the jewellery exhibition. They might ring to find out why she hadn't come and when the phone wasn't answered they would shrug and forget her. There were the people who were to call with her new chairs—when they had no answer to their knocking they would shrug and forget her. They would say to one another that she would call or ring them in her own good time and that would be that.

There was no-one who would jump to the conclusion that something was wrong; no-one who would fret and worry over her. Somehow that was the worst thing about the whole situation—that in the world there was no-one to whom she was vitally necessary; no-one who couldn't do without her and would come searching for her if she was missing for only a short time.

She pushed that thought aside because it was unbearable and went on concentrating on the petty orderly details of her life, searching for someone who might possibly miss her doing some trifle and comment on it.

There was Wing Lee in the restaurant next door where she ate once or twice a week. Would he . . .

Wing Lee, she thought.

She crouched down again, looking at the blank space in the wall. Beyond it was the dark cavity interior of the wall, then another brick and then the inside of Wing Lee's.

She nearly laughed at the absurdity of it, at the thought that all along she had been separated from the world, from other people, from the scents and warmth of the restaurant, by a single brick. She reached for the heeled slipper again and wondered how long it would take her to push the brick out,

157

reflecting on the shrill cries, the excitement, the flurry and wonder, when in a little while, her hand, the nails torn, the skin bloodied and scratched, came through the wall, grasping for comfort and help.

And then she knew it wasn't going to happen. Because with her hand outstretched the slipper could just touch the brick the other side of the cavity. She couldn't, because of the shelves in the vault, reach close enough to gouge and pry at the brick and force a way through.

CHAPTER FOURTEEN

STEPHEN came out of the area, closing the lane gate with a bang and as though it had been a signal long waited for, the woman appeared in the end of the lane. When she saw him frown lines grew across her forehead under the green scarf and she turned, beginning to hurry away again.

He called, "Mrs. Swan," and reluctantly, one foot still in front of the other as though she were poised for flight, she stopped, turning towards him again.

She said hurriedly, "I came to see Miss Penghill. When I heard the squeaking gate . . ."

"She isn't home. She's gone into the city to a jewellery exhibition," he told her. Then lightly, almost teasingly, because of the growing frown, he asked, "Any more trouble? Any more phone-calls? Any . . ."

"That's what I wanted to see Miss Penghill about. Oh, I don't mean there's been another phone-call and if there had been I'd have been on to the police by this time. Oh no, it's not that at all. But last night—my husband, you know, said I shouldn't start in worrying Mrs. Penghill because there's nothing really to be done, but I thought someone . . . of the family, if you see what I mean . . . should know. I didn't like going to his office. Mr. Penghill's, I mean. I just thought that if I mentioned my idea to Miss Penghill that . . . she sounded so sensible last night!" she suddenly burst out.

Watching her he knew that she was seeking some sort of reassurance, some settlement of the worry that was causing the deep frown lines across her forehead. He said so, bluntly, and saw the deep flush rush into her pale cheeks.

Then she said, "It's just that I don't want it on my

conscience if something . . . if there was any trouble. You see, I think it was Ann that man wanted. Maybe I'm wrong, but . . . he was looking for a child . . ."

She poured it all out the way she had poured it out to Fred Swan in the night. He listened silently till all the worry had run out of her and she was calm again and then he said definitely, "You're wrong. The man who rang you wasn't at the English place, and at the Penghills'. Sandy Micklin was lured outside by a man who rang her, saying he was a neighbour, asking her to go out and search for a lost dog. And he took her to be Mrs. Penghill and spoke to her by that name.

"He thought Roger Penghill was away and that Mrs. Penghill was there alone with Ann. The same sort of thing as at the English house—Mr. English was away. His wife was there alone."

Her lips parted in surprise. He knew she was finding it difficult to discard her theory, to think of two men instead of one.

Then she said, "It was him mentioning the reserve, you see. He said he'd seen Judy in the reserve, only she hasn't been there for over a fortnight and it wasn't Lynette English because she has chicken-pox. But Ann was there with her class this last Wednesday. I got that from the school. Judy wasn't there that day though. Only Ann out of the three of them went."

"With her class? How many children in the class have long or longish hair? Hair that could be described as light brown?" he wondered aloud for her benefit. "People think of different shades when they hear that. It would depend on what sort of light the child was in, too. I've heard light brown describing anything short of dark hair down to a dulled blonde."

"You're right," she admitted after a little thought.

"And whoever rang the Penghills wanted to speak to Deidre Penghill," he told her. "He never so much as mentioned Ann. I shouldn't worry about it. Whatever your chap had in mind when he rang Judy he'll be scared off for now. There's been too much publicity—people will be too alert to let their infants at the phone."

He saw the easing of her expression and went on reassuring her as he walked a few steps with her, offering her a lift to wherever she was going.

Neither of them looked back at the closed shop.

. . .

Though it was impossible to use the steel shank of the slipper's heel to gouge and pry the brick of Wing Lee's wall loose from its mortar there was still hope.

She realised that only slowly, long after she had tried to still the shivering of her body, the complete despair that had settled down on her mind, by reminding herself that she had no idea what was beyond the brick—that almost certainly the wall in the café wasn't like the one in the vault—with the bare bricks whitewashed over. Possibly it was plastered, maybe panelled, maybe with fitments built on to it. She had tried remembering the inside of the place, sure there was wooden panelling somewhere that she had idly noted once or twice, but she had found an odd dream-like state to her picturings, as though she was conjuring up, not a picture of something real and tangible, but something that existed only in imagination.

The same dream-like state seemed to belong to everything— one after another she tried visualising her old rooms at the other end of the town; the new showroom; the interior of the Penghill house on Acacia Way. All of them, known inch by inch, held the same air of unreality now to her thoughts. The fact frightened her, worried her, left her wondering if the dream-like state would grow till the real world was lost to her; that this oddness of memory and visualisation was a warning that time was running out and soon she would let the craving for sleep that was nagging at her take complete hold of her and she would sink down onto the vault's floor and simply not get up again.

It was the panic and fear that came with that idea

161 UN—K

that gave new strength to her thoughts, seeking a way of escape.

And then she realised there was still hope.

Because she had only to bang on the wall and sooner or later she was going to be heard. Perhaps, she warned herself, wriggling into position on the floor of the vault, taking a purchase on the heeled slipper, striving for space in which to swing so that the slipper would hit the wall with as much force as possible, it wouldn't be heard—not really hard and commented on—for a fair while. At first it might be just a niggling noise they would expect to go away. But later on, someone was going to come close to the wall. Sooner or later someone was going to notice the regularity of the bangs—five in a row and then silence and then five more.

And they'd get help.

She lay there, carefully counting, swinging rhythmically, sweat pricking at her skin even with that faint exertion, the torture of thirst resolutely fought down together with the craving for sleep. She thought instead of Wing Lee and his fat little wife and the steaming plates of noodles and fish, topped with juicy orange segments, that were the café's speciality.

She dwelt on them, forcing herself to concentrate, as she counted and swung and tapped and banged, on every aspect that must go into the preparation and cooking of her favourite dishes, while outside, the wind was picking up again, gently turning and twisting at the white notice on the café door, on which was lettered, "Closed Mondays".

· · ·

Stephen asked, "What's your betting on it?"

Giddings accepted a cigarette from the proffered packet and shrugged his big shoulders. "He won't make it, and for my money St. Peter's welcome to him. It'll save us a lot of work and trouble."

The younger man grinned, suggesting, "Not St. Peter surely?"

"I went to a politician's funeral once," Giddings mused. "According to the clergyman's piece the bloke was a candidate for wings. If he could've got in why not you and me and Deeford?" He added bluntly, "I've got nothing to give you. And I've work to do."

"I wanted to know if you'd had anything about more prowlers? And phone pests?"

'What d'you expect? Every fool woman in town's been on the phone since your piece went over the air. If every place that had someone snooping round really had 'em the bloke must have had a jet engine tied to his tail to get him around. As for phone pests—you wouldn't believe the number of respectable women that've . . ."

"I wouldn't," Stephen broke in. "And you don't, either. I should think our man was scared off and went home after the episode at Penghills'—he might have been badly scratched by the cat. Did you think of that? The brute has claws like the devil—I've had them in myself."

Giddings grunted. "If you think I've got nothing better to do than chase round town looking for scratches . . ."

"I was thinking of mentioning it in my session. You never know, it might turn someone up."

"Too right—half a dozen poor coots that've scratched their mugs for other reasons and have to hot-foot it here for protection against irate women who've heard you." He scowled at the other's chuckle.

"That reminds me, did my call last night turn up anyone who'd been in the reserve?" Stephen questioned.

"No. No-one's been near us today either. Didn't expect it. It's the sort of case decent people'd want to be clear of. There was someone in the reserve though right enough—we found fresh picnic scraps and a kid's drawing-book. Ten to one the folks who left them ran for it when the rain started. Which was just after Deeford tossed the girl in the water." He sighed, reaching irritably for the top sheet of the pile of papers in

163

front of him. "Not that it matters now. If Deeford pulls through we ought to get enough on him. I was going to ask at the school who owned the book—though I might get a lead that way to some adult who saw him and Rose together. But," his shoulders moved again, dismissing the idea, "there's no need at the moment. I doubt if he'll pull through."

· · ·

It was mid-afternoon when she finally stopped and thirst and the need for sleep became something of such urgency it could no longer be ignored.

She crouched there, the torn and scratched slipper beside her, her hand still on the lighter that she had clicked on so she could see the time.

Mid-afternoon, she thought stupidly, and asked herself uselessly, over and over again, how it was possible that they hadn't heard her banging—five knocks in a row and then silence, time after time.

There seemed to her tired and sweating body, less air than ever in the vault. She bent forwards with her face towards the gap in the brickwork, though she knew that crouching there, banging on the wall across the black cavity, she had been breathing all the time at what air there was.

She tried inching forward, tried to peer into the blackness, flicking the lighter flame into action again, trying to light the inside of the cavity, then sharply she drew back. It was imagination she was sure, but for a minute there seemed faint pricks of light in the blackness, as though the light had caught tiny eyes watching her. She had thought that, she was certain, simply because the remembrance of the rat had jumped back into her thoughts.

But the brute had scuttled away into some hole in the foundations of the building. She crouched there, numbly speculating on the rat, wondering how it had dared, even after the noise of her earlier banging had ceased, to come staring at her, an enemy; wondering why the workaday noises of the world around the block hadn't driven all the vermin in the place into hiding places during the daylight.

And then suddenly remembrance was clear and she cried out with the pain of it, knowing why the rat had dared, why it was busily moving around in the cavity walls. It was because there was silence from her place and silence from Wing Lee's.

Silence from the place where she had hoped and striven to get help. The futility of all she had done, all the tiring knocking, five knocks at a time and then pause, over and over again, brought tears trickling down her face, slowly, soundlessly.

There had been only the rats to hear all her knocking and bangings all the day long.

She crouched there, remembering that Wing Lee stayed open till late on Saturday evening and the café opened on Sundays for Sunday dinner too, in the hope of catching weekend trippers along the highway. And from then, from the time things were cleared away, some time in the afternoon, the place was closed—till Tuesday morning. For Wing Lee and his small fat wife Monday was their sabbath, their one day of rest in all the week. And the place was a lock-up shop—they didn't live above it.

The tears went on rolling slowly down her face while her body rocked, trying to ease the pain the memory brought, trying to still the despair of knowing that now she couldn't expect help till some time in the morning.

Then suddenly she wasn't crying, or crouching, or even thinking. There was only blankness and blackness again and a sleep that wiped out everything.

And just as suddenly she was awake again, knowing that the rat was back. That it was actually in the vault with her.

．　　　．　　　．

The florist's wasn't busy. Sandy was on the phone when he came in and by the blush he could see rising up under the heavy make-up on her young face, he guessed that she and

165

Lloyd Thompson were killing the idle time in both the shop and at the garage.

She said brightly, "Yes, Mr. Linquist?"

"I don't want flowers, Sandy," he said and saw the brightness fade out of her face.

"You're not going to go on at me about last night are you?" She was immediately on the defensive. "Because . . ."

"I just wanted to ask you one thing. Do you think that cat of the Penghills scratched your prowler?"

It was a new thought to her, he could tell. She simply stared for a moment, then burst out, "I hope it did!"

"You didn't notice blood on its claws then?"

She gave him a quick look that was half mocking, half humorous. "Mr. Linquist, if he'd had diamonds on his paws I wouldn't have noticed. All I was noticing was the way my knees were knocking." Then abruptly, bluntly, she added, "I thought you didn't believe me anyway. You didn't believe me last night. Did you?"

"No."

Her finger traced a little circle in a patch of water on the counter. "Then what's changed your mind?" she challenged.

"Lloyd telling me that it was Mrs. Penghill the man thought he was speaking to. If your story was made up you'd have left that out."

She nodded, then challenged again, "How long are you going on at me about it? Because I want to forget it."

"You can do that whenever you like, Sandy. I only wanted to know about the cat because I thought of mentioning it in my session tonight."

Her eyes rounded. "Yes, I get it. Someone might've noticed someone who'd . . ." she broke off, then asked, "What's the latest about Rose and her trouble? I know her, you know. We went to school together. It's all over town the man at Spencers is the man who . . ."

"Martin Deeford? Yes, it's no secret."

Her eyes were bright and expectant. "I said to Lloyd last night it was funny — I mean, we'd been to see Rose, you see and she wouldn't say much, but she let drop he had golden hair. It didn't make me any wiser . . . not then. Only I said to Lloyd that was funny because of Miss Penghill asking about a man with golden hair and I said to Lloyd what if she saw him somewhere doing something funny, because it was just after she'd told me about that pest ringing Judith Swan. Just as though one funny sort made her remember another one, like. Why'd she ask me that?" The expectancy was growing as she leaned towards him.

He gazed back blankly. "Rachel Penghill asked you about a golden-haired man? What did she ask about him?"

"Just did I know who he was and I didn't. But it seemed like to me as though speaking of one odd sort had . . . why'd she ask me?"

He shook his head. "I haven't the devil's notion, Sandy."

She pouted her disappointment. "I thought maybe I'd see her round today and could ask because she buys flowers Mondays usually, only today she's never been in."

"She's gone to a jewellery exhibition," he spoke absently, then smiled at her. "Put a few things together, Sandy. The sort of thing she usually buys. I'll take them round to her tonight."

He watched her slim hands moving among the few late autumn flowers, adding sprays of leaves, twisting the lot into pink tissue paper.

As she handed it to him she asked, "Are you going to ask her why she questioned me about him?"

"I expect so." Then he said abruptly, "But I think I can make a pretty good guess as to why she asked. According to the police, after Deeford dealt with Rose he was somewhere in town for quite a while. I should think he had plenty of fear and panic to work off. He probably did it by burning up the deserted roads on that scooter of his, getting up enough courage to go home and act as though nothing had happened. And Rachel saw him."

She gave a jerk of laughter. "And here was me imagining all sorts of things."

"Heavy drama, Sandy?" He laughed with her, paid for the flowers and said good night to her, but when he reached the end shop and rang at the bell there was only silence.

He was suddenly glad of it. If she had been in, there would have been time for little more than giving her the flowers and having a few brief words before he would have to hurry away again. He would, he decided, going back to the car and placing the flowers carefully on the back seat, come back after his session that night. She'd be relaxed after her trip then, perhaps content to talk a while; there'd be a companionable cup of coffee, firelight, with her in the chair opposite him.

He cursed himself for the thought. He told himself he didn't want any of it, not Rachel's deep voice speaking in a quiet firelit room, or her gaze on his, a mood of relaxation and a peace, a companionship, that tugged at his heart, urging him to ask her to marry him and to hell with the consequences of it.

He decided, starting the car moving, that he wasn't going to risk it. He wasn't going back in the quiet lateness of the evening. He would call in some time in the morning if he had time and give her the flowers then. If not, they could go to his landlady.

.   .   .

There had been soft sounds, a faint movement near her face, barely enough to disturb her senses but she had known quite definitely the rat was there, in the vault with her. Her hand went out scrabbling frantically for the lighter, and touched softness that moved.

She screamed and went on screaming. The sound tore from her, echoing round the vault, and she couldn't stop, not till suddenly there seemed no sound left in her and there was only the agony of her sore, thirst-racked throat and silence.

When she finally found the lighter and flicked it on, moving the light so that she could see as much of the vault as possible, gingerly moving the rumbled trays, she knew it had disappeared into the cavity wall and back into its hole somewhere in the foundations of the building.

But she knew quite definitely she wouldn't be courageous enough to sleep again if it and others like it could reach her. There were headlines flaring in memory—Child Attacked, Baby Bitten in Cot—that wouldn't go away and she was left with the sickening imaginings of herself asleep and waking to the viciousness of a rat biting into her own flesh.

Desperately she told herself not to be a fool. She croaked the words aloud, reminding herself that she was an adult—not a helpless baby. She'd wake and be able to fight the brute off. But the thought of it attacking her was still something to bring rising panic. The very idea of it touching her, moving across her body was revolting. And how many rats were there down under the building? How many might come flooding through the cavity in the wall to attack her?

She knew that she wasn't going to be able to sleep again while there was a way free to them to get at her, but sleep was still an overwhelming, imperative need, and an escape from the thirst that was a searing pain in her throat, and the despair and panic that was there at the back of her mind, waiting for a chance to flare into uncontrolled hysteria.

Flicking the lighter on again, seeing it was nearly six o'clock, she was surprised, because she had seemed to have slept for no time at all. The passing unconscious hours had certainly brought her no new strength. She was desperately tired, and even moving her arm so she could see the watch, bending her head towards it in the light of the tiny flame was an effort so great it frightened her because it was a reminder of growing weakness.

She tried convincing herself that in the morning, after his holiday, Wing Lee would make an early start. A very early one. There would be goods arriving for the day's trade and the cooking to start. What if he came at six o'clock? she wondered. It wasn't impossible. And that would mean only twelve hours.

"*Only,*" she thought, and suddenly there seemed a monstrous lifetime to be fought through in her gradually weakening state.

I'm not going to think of it, she said aloud and her trembling hands reached and groped and found the brick she had discarded, lifted it and managed to ease it back into the hole in the wall, then she lay back, panting, sweat pricking again at her skin, wooing sleep this time, glad when it came.

But then waking to the airlessness of the vault, to a feeling of suffocation, to a frantic, finger-tearing pulling at the brick, a gasping and crying as it wouldn't move and had to be prised out with the help of the steel shank in her slipper, undid any good that the sleep might have brought her.

She lay down, breathing deeply of the musty dank air that came to her, wondering how it happened that before she had survived a long time of the vault's air before feeling so ill, yet this time it had been a matter of two hours. She knew that, after groping and flicking on the lighter again. But she knew the answer even while her tired brain was probing at the question. It was because she was growing steadily weaker, her body less able to cope with any strain. And she was going to grow weaker. There was no use trying to deny that.

But at six o'clock, or seven, or eight, or nine at the very latest, Wing Lee will be next door, she reminded herself and wondered how long it would be after that before he heard her and did something about it.

Eight o'clock, she decided. He was coming at eight o'clock. Not six after all. That was too early and she'd be only disappointed and sink into despair when he didn't come. She would try at eight o'clock to attract his attention. Till then she was going to remain calm. She was going to sleep a little with the brick in place, and then remove it and get what air she could. And sleep again.

Eight o'clock, she thought again, centring her mind on it, deciding what she would have to eat and drink when she was free, planning a brief holiday, centring her mind definitely on a pleasant future so that the fear that was there wasn't going to be any future didn't creep back on her to shatter the last of her control.

CHAPTER FIFTEEN

Ann woke to the pleasant knowledge that there was something unusual and exciting about the day. She lay there for several moments, blinking against the pillow, dredging into memory and recollection to find what it was the day held.

When Deidre Penghill came in, still in a rose-coloured wrapper, to say brightly, "Up you get, Ann, morning's here," she rolled over and said:

"Mummy, last night . . ."

"Wasn't it nice of Mr. and Mrs. Guen to call in like that?" Deidre knew her tone was falsely bright and she grimaced at the sound of it as she paused on her way back to the door. The unexpected visit of the Guens had been a bore and an irritation, but one didn't, she reasoned wryly, admit so much to a nine-year-old—a gabby nine-year-old, as Roger would say—who would repeat the remarks to all and sundry and hurt the Guens' all too sensitive feelings for ever more.

Ann said somewhat severely, "I wanted to talk to you, but they stayed and stayed . . ."

And stayed, and how, Deidre reflected, even while she smiled and said, "They had lots of things to talk about too. What was it you wanted, pet?"

"About . . ." Ann hesitated, then went on sturdily, "About what happened on Sunday. It was all in the papers," she pointed out breathlessly, "and I read it and it said in the reserve on Sunday and mummy . . ." she saw Deidre's frown and stopped.

Deidre's fingers tapped nervously on the edge of the bed, then she said, "I expect you have to know sooner or later that

. . . nasty things happen. You know what I've told you about there being people . . ."

"But Mummy," Ann was impatient now. She hunched up in the small bed, her face eager, "*I* was in the reserve on Sunday. That's where we went. And on Sunday night Mr. Linquist asked for anyone who'd been in the reserve and I wondered why, only when I said about it yesterday you wouldn't listen. And then last night in the paper I saw all about that girl and the man and I wanted to tell you only . . ." she broke off again, alarmed at the whiteness, the dismay in Deidre's expression.

"You were in the reserve? Aunt Rachel took you . . . ?"

"Yes."

"Ann," Deidre sat down heavily on the edge of the bed, "What . . . did you see anyone? I mean, did you see this girl?"

There was clear regret in Ann's, "No. We didn't see anyone at all. It was all quiet and there was only us. But we were there. Right in the reserve."

Deidre stood up again. She said, "Well, you're not to say so. Do you understand that? You're not to mention it to a soul." Her voice rose. "We don't want to get mixed up in a case like that. We'll have all sorts of people poking and prying and wanting to make you say this and that . . . you're not to say a word. Understand?" At the child's slow, disappointed nod, her expression changed. She said more lightly, "And after all there was nothing you saw, was there? Aunt Rachel was away all day yesterday or I expect she would have called in and told me. I expect I'll see her today. Or tomorrow. But she won't talk about it to anyone, I know. And you're not to, either. Promise?"

Reluctantly, because a splendid chance of being the centre of attention, like Sandy, was sliding out of her grasp, Ann gave in.

·　　·　　·

173

At five o'clock she had suddenly thought of the dog. She had never given it a name; never tried to claim it as her own in spite of her fussings over it. She had known quite well that she didn't want it to adopt her as its mistress, because she had been hoping, still hoping that Stephen would ask her to go away with him and then the dog would have had to be left behind. And she'd wanted no regrets, no pangs of conscience.

She had fed it, and dosed it and given it shelter, and she had been sure that it had sensed in her something withheld. It had never fawned on her, nor tried to get inside the house. It had simply accepted what she chose to give it and that was as far as their relationship had gone.

They had been friends. Slightly wary friends, she thought in wry amusement. It had been much the same relationship as between herself and Stephen in fact. Friendship given, but something, something important, forever withheld.

But the dog, she realised, hadn't been fed since Sunday. At first there had been wild hope in the thought. She had pictured it whining and howling outside the closed shop, scratching at the door, drawing attention to the fact that she was missing. Then the hope had gone. The relationship between them was such that she was sure nothing of the sort would happen. She had shown the animal that she was independent, owing him nothing and expecting nothing in return. If she didn't appear again he might hang round for a little, then he would simply lope away to try and find another home, and forget her.

So there wasn't so much as a dog who would miss her.

It was a horrible thought that in her weakened state seemed like the final straw, the final cruelty of fate.

She crouched on the vault's floor, trying to forget the animal completely, to banish the whole thought of him and his lack of feeling for her, from her mind. The night had brought despair enough without her thinking of the dog. There had been sleep and terrible awakening to a feeling of suffocation, and more sleep and another awakening, and each time the sleep had been a little less and the awakening more painful.

And she had, she told herself, only to wait till someone came into the restaurant and then she was going to be heard and later she would be safe.

When she was quite sure, in spite of listening hopefully for sounds and hearing nothing, that there must be someone in the restaurant beyond the far wall, she started to knock again. Five knocks and then a hopeful silence.

It took a long time, till her body was completely exhausted and her arm simply failed to function any more before she gave up, and simply lay there, striving for new energy, for new hope.

She thought then of other headlines she had seen in past newspapers — stories of milkmen who brought help to aged and injured people, because a tell-tale line of milk bottles was outside their closed door, and she wondered what the milkman had thought that morning when he had found yesterday's filled bottle on her step.

There had been a brief flash of hope in that till she had thought that perhaps he had simply shrugged and gone away. He wouldn't have left another, because there was no empty bottle, no money, for him to collect. But if he hadn't shrugged — if he went into the café and asked about her, concerned for her?

Hope had slid away again. She remembered telling Wing Lee's fat little wife that she was going away. She strove in memory to try and remember if she had said how long she would be away. She couldn't remember at all. But she had definitely told the little woman she was going away to the jewellery exhibition. And she had said that Timson had the key and was going to carry out work while she was gone. She remembered that clearly because the little woman had been interested in the redecoration of the place and they had discussed the stairs and the work Timson was going to do.

So if the milkman made inquiries about her, Wing Lee's

little wife was going to say simply that she was away, and that would be that. They'd think she had forgotten all about the milk and meant to be away two days, or three, or four.

They wouldn't do anything. They wouldn't miss her.

And then hope slid away finally and completely. She thought of that conversation with Wing Lee's wife and there was nothing left in her but exhaustion and defeat.

Because she had told the little woman Timson was going to work in the place. So any sound, any knocking, any hammering from her place wasn't going to be answered from the restaurant. She could knock and knock, beat on the wall for all she was worth and they were going to nod and say to each other how nice it was that the work was finally being completed.

And no-one was going to do a thing to help her.

.　　　.　　　.

Stephen questioned hopefully, "Any statement?"

"Not a thing." Giddings closed the folder in front of him with a little slam. "I didn't expect it. He was too badly burned. Mostly his legs and the lower part of his body, poor bastard. And his hands. Trying to save himself. His face wasn't hurt, funnily enough, except for Rose's efforts. She got her nails into him all right." He heaved a gusty sigh. "But that's the finish of him and the finish of our job. We can forget all about it. I bet," he added cynically, "our Rose'll be fit to be tied. No court case, no publicity, no posing for the papers, no nothing, because he went and died too soon. Poor Rose."

"Your crocodile tears are showing," Stephen said absently. "By the way, I think I know what he was doing in the time between putting her in the lake and sneaking home before running for it. He was burning up the roads round town. And made himself conspicuous. At least I think a friend of mine saw him and wondered what he was up to."

"That so? I had half an idea he might have been trying a smash and grab somewhere to get money to help him do a flit.

The police up north thought he was muttering about a vault. Of course it was Rose Gault he was really chatting about, but I did think of the other thing. There's been no report come in of trouble though." He cocked an eyebrow, "Who's the friend saw him?"

Stephen hesitated, then said shortly, "Rachel Penghill."

"The opal girl? I bought one of her things for my wife last anniversary. The wife was tickled pink." He suddenly grinned, "I've a drawing of your girl here somewhere . . ."

He reached among the papers and pulled out a brown paper-covered book. It was draggled and dirty, but he turned the pages, finally slapping the open book down in front of the younger man, so that Stephen was staring at a drawing of Rachel. It was quite clearly her, even capturing her smile. But it wasn't the drawing itself that interested him, as much as the book, that he recognised as Ann's. The child was rarely without it. He said absently, "I'll be in there somewhere too. Not recognisably. I look bull-headed and bad-tempered . . ."

"You know who owns it?"

"Yes, Ann Penghill. Why?"

"The solicitor's kid?"

"Yes. Where did you get hold of it?"

"Remember me telling you I found a drawing-book in the reserve on Sunday? That's it."

Stephen looked up sharply, then he grinned, "Just as well you didn't have it fixed as a clue. The book wasn't lost Sunday. Ann was there last Wednesday though."

Giddings scowled. "Trying to teach me my business? That book wasn't there Wednesday. Poured all day Thursday. The book would have been pulp. It wasn't even wet through completely when I got it Sunday. And it was right beside those picnic scraps—and they hadn't been there longer than a few hours. So?"

Stephen was lost in frowning abstraction, then he gave a little snap of his fingers, "So that's where Rachel saw him. Not in the town. In the reserve?" questioningly, as though Giddings could tell him.

The sergeant shrugged. "Why ask me? I wouldn't know."

The younger man didn't hear him. He was saying slowly, "That must be it, you know. She must have taken Ann there and seen him—she asked Sandy if the kid knew a golden-haired man and Sandy wondered . . . I wonder what the devil he was doing, looking like, to make Rachel notice him so particularly?"

"If you're going to tell me she saw him throw Rose in the lake and said to herself, 'How very odd' and then went home, I don't believe you." Giddings rumbled with sudden laughter, then he asked sharply, almost angrily, "Why didn't she come forward to say she'd been down there?"

"I don't expect she knew anything about it. She's been away at some exhibition."

Giddings nodded, "And ten to one the kiddy doesn't know tuppence about it. I doubt her mum'd let her read the news-paper dirt. And what the hell, anyway—it doesn't matter now. He's dead and the case is closed. Just as well you know—your girl friend wouldn't relish getting a summons to court and Penghill'd have a fit if we started questioning his kid. Wouldn't he?"

Stephen said shortly, standing up, "She's not my girl friend as it happens," and because he didn't want the statement questioned, smiled at, commented on, he changed the subject.

Only when he left the building did he think of it again, promising himself he'd see Rachel that evening and ask her about the time she'd seen Deeford.

But there were other things more important. Seeing Rose Gault for instance. Mr. and Mrs. Public Citizen, he thought wryly, were going to want to know Rose's feeling on learning of Deeford's death, so he had to get them and serve them up with appropriate editing. Tripe, garnished with parsley, he thought disgustedly, and was suddenly glad that in a few more days he would be finished with the town for good—that in the future there'd be no more of the Rose sort of interviews. From next week he'd be plunged into news that was history.

. . .

Rose said sullenly, "I'm not sorry," and leaned back on her pillows. She was still at home, still determinedly revelling in the invalidism, the attention, that she felt was called for after her ordeal. "And that sort," she added with finality, "aren't fit to live."

He said mildly, "That's not going to sound pretty to other people, Rose. They haven't experienced the sort of ordeal you have. They'll remember only that Mart was very young and . . ."

Cynically he watched her, seeing the calculation going on behind her young eyes.

She said sharply, "I know. But I've a right to be angry and bitter, haven't I? I'm sorry enough for him in a way, and I'm right sorry," her tone was suddenly sugared with emotion as she lowered her lashes, "for his family. His sister. I'm just terribly sorry about her."

He was suddenly tired of her. He said curtly, "Anyway, you put up a good fight, didn't you, Rose? You marked his face badly with your nails."

Her blackened lashes flicked up in surprise. "Who're you kidding? Me scratch him? Like fanny I did."

"He was badly scratched." He frowned at her.

"Wasn't me," her cheeks were flushed. "Go and sneer all you like, but have a look."

He looked at the bitten, distorted nails and grimaced. They were so badly bitten she couldn't have scratched anyone, so Mart must have scratched his face in the accident someway, falling on to something . . .

She broke across his thoughts with a sharp, "Say, you don't mean he might've got smart with someone else and got scratched, do you?" She shook her head, "But no-one's

179

squawked, have they? I guess," her tone was sour, "he got it kicking the cat. I bet he was just the type'd kick the cat hard. Hey, what're you staring at?" she demanded impatiently.

He came out of abstraction, and shook his head. "I was thinking."

He got away as quickly as he could, but once in the car he didn't drive away, though he knew she and her mother were probably peering at him from behind the curtains. He was thinking of Deeford's scratched face and the Penghills' cat. And Rachel having seen Deeford and asking Sandy about him.

Had it been near the Penghill house she had seen him? Not in the reserve at all? Or perhaps in both places? It was certainly an odd coincidence—if it was that—that someone who might have been badly scratched had been at the Penghills', and Mart Deeford had had unaccounted scratches on his face.

He was suddenly thinking of something else—of Agnes Swan, her face furrowed with worry, talking of a man who was apparently trying to find a child with long hair. Long light brown hair. A child who had been in the reserve. But the man hadn't spoken of seeing the child on Wednesday, had he? And why had he waited till the Sunday to try and find her?

What if he had been looking for a child seen in the reserve that Sunday? For Ann Penghill in fact? Had it been Martin Deeford who had rung the Swan house, and later at the Penghills' . . .

But it didn't add up, he thought impatiently. The man had thought Sandy was Deidre Penghill. He hadn't mentioned Ann. And there was the English case. He had tried getting the woman outside there . . .

The woman, he thought. He had, both times, tried to get the woman alone. He had been looking for a woman then? A woman who had been with a child in the reserve? Had he been trying to find her through the child?

Mrs. English, he remembered, had told him she'd gone to the back door and looked out and gone a few steps out. She hadn't gone searching the place till later. The man was gone then. And then he had turned up at the Penghill place. Why hadn't he waited in the hope Mrs. English would finally come out searching as she had done, in fact.

Why, unless he had seen her in the light and known she wasn't the one he wanted?

I'm getting fanciful, he thought impatiently. Mrs. Swan wasn't lured out. He didn't see her at all. But he didn't go back there. Why? If I'm right.

Then he thought, "But Agnes Swan spoke to him."

Could that mean the man was looking for a woman who'd been in the reserve with a child and had spoken to him, so that he knew her both by voice and by sight?

He thought of the episode at the Penghill house. Had the cat really frightened the man away as everyone thought? Or had he left because he had realised Sandy, too, wasn't the woman he wanted? He remembered her saying she had fallen to the ground. Why hadn't the man shaken off the cat and attacked her while she was helpless?

It was mad, he thought impatiently, and yet there was a queer streak of reality in it that could be added together. He took every facet of it, fitting it neatly into place putting Martin Deeford into the position of the man who had been active through that unquiet Sunday night.

Deeford had dealt with Rose. Start with that, he thought. Then he had been seen and spoken to by a woman in the reserve. A woman with a child. And then what? The rain had come. The three of them had gone different ways. And had Deeford then realised the woman was a danger to him? But what about the child? There had been no attempt to attack children. He told himself that obviously then the child hadn't seen Deeford or spoken to him. Only the woman had. But the man had seen both of them.

He had realised the danger too late and had then tried to find the woman. He had got the names of Judith and Lynette from Miss Thatcher, tracing the woman the only way he knew how—through the child. He had spoken to Mrs. Swan and known she wasn't the woman he was seeking. He had seen Mrs. English and left that house too. And then . . . how had he got the Penghills' name?

That was a point that needed clearing up, but he had turned up there, if this strangely real, yet impossible story was correct. And he had lured Sandy out, believing her to be Mrs. Penghill.

He thought suddenly how alike Ann and Rachel were—so alike they would easily be taken for mother and daughter.

So Sandy was lured out. And knocked down. And Deeford had left without hurting her, but he himself had been badly scratched by the Siamese cat.

And then what? He sat on, smoking, fitting the last pieces into the puzzle.

Deeford hadn't planned flight. He had meant to deal with the woman who had seen him, and then he would have been safe. But after going to the Penghill house he had run out of clues. He had known he couldn't find the woman and so he had fled.

He remembered what time it had been Sandy was lured out. The time would be fairly correct, he reflected—just about time for Deeford to have reached the point he did before his accident.

He felt suddenly sick, thinking of Rachel being hunted through the night. He tried to tell himself that the whole story was probably a lot of nonsense. But he knew that he had to see Rachel. At once. And find out where she had seen Deeford and when, and what had happened between them. He had to talk it all over with her and then perhaps he could laugh at himself for the panic and fear that was touching him now.

· · ·

It was as though the final despair had brought a calm acceptance, a new courage. She crouched there, going over each trivial detail of her life, discarding them one by one with the same calm acceptance of her failure to find in them a way out.

There was Timson. He might come by the end of the week. She doubted if he would come before. There was the milkman who might possibly go to the café, only to be reassured. There was Wing Lee and his wife who would, in their sweet politeness — the politeness she had so often warmed to — never dream of questioning where she was; never dream of knocking on her door and wondering at the silence; never dream of commenting on noises from her building. There was Stephen who would perhaps knock and then go away with a mind full of relief because time was running out and he was getting away from her without an emotional goodbye. There was Roger and Deidre who wouldn't miss her — till the shop failed to open on schedule. There were dozens of people who might send in bills that would slide through the mail slot in her door, scattering on the lino beyond, and even if she was missing for a couple of months they would do nothing more about it than send further bills with little red-inked reminders at the bottom of the sheets.

There was the dog who would soon go away and find another home and forget her.

She discarded them all and then she knew she was simply going to sleep. In sleep she was going to find oblivion from despair and thirst and hunger and the terrible knowledge that she was so tiny, so unimportant a cog in the world that she could disappear without comment.

Her hands sought the brick and clumsily, slowly, she fitted it into the gap in the wall. Then she lay down, the blue robe pulled round her body, and sleep was there, and accepted.

CHAPTER SIXTEEN

THAT there was no answer to his ringing was suddenly a flaring irritation. He stood back from the shop front, staring up at the windows of the flat and there was suddenly a stab of apprehension, of panic, in his mind, because in that brilliant sunshine of mid-day the curtains over his head were tightly drawn.

Sharply he moved into the side lane and saw the dog again. It came forward, snuffling at his shoes, looking at him with hopeful eyes. He bent to pat it, asking "Have you been fed?" and knowing that either it had been let out or it had jumped the low fence between the back of Rachel's place and the small lane.

He opened the gate and went in and stood frowning. The water dish was bone dry again and the other dish was empty, too, beside it and there were empty wrappings of the meat he had brought the previous day.

He said to the dog, and there was anxiety in his voice, "Where is she?" and he knew he was afraid, and the fear was simply because of the story he had built up. Out of fairy floss he told himself furiously. Out of that and nothing more. What was he getting into a panic about, for heaven's sake?

Why imagine that Deeford had really been after Rachel and that after leaving the Penghill house that Sunday night he had someway found her and . . . his mind refused to dwell on the thought of what might have followed.

But the idea was crazy, insane, he thought impatiently. Why let drawn curtains and an unfed dog start his mind playing tricks? Rachel had gone to an exhibition, hadn't she?

And gratefully he suddenly remembered that whatever had

happened on Sunday night in the town, on Monday Rachel had been all right. He remembered the milk on her doorstep and that later, when he had fed the dog, it had gone. Rachel had overslept then and left in a hurry. And stayed overnight in town, for a certainty.

He said to the dog, "I'll be back," and later when he had fed it he went into Wing Lee's and ordered fish and noodles, remembering sitting there with Rachel opposite him, eating the same dish. When the little smiling Chinese woman brought the food he asked her, "Mrs. Wing, do you know where Miss Penghill is?"

She beamed, said in her almost accentless voice, "In the city."

"She hasn't come back yet?"

"Not yet, I think."

"You don't know when she's expected back then?"

Her little dark eyes regarded him smilingly, almost teasingly. He felt himself reddening under the scrutiny, remembering the way she clucked over the pair of them when they ate together, obviously hoping and waiting for some romance to blossom between then.

She said gently, "Perhaps you ask Mr. Timson and he might say."

"Mr. Timson?" he probed.

She nodded vigorously, "He has key to work in there. Very busy man all morning, hammering." She smiled, hurrying away to attend to another customer, leaving him to relish the food as best he could without Rachel's conversation, her gentle smile, the warmth in her eyes, to sweeten it. And suddenly it was as sour as leaf ash in his mouth.

It was then a question came darting into his mind. Why hadn't Timson, if he was working in Rachel's place, answered the ringing at the door?

He went with quick strides out of the café, knowing that Mrs. Wing was staring after him in astonishment. He went up to the closed door of the jewellery shop, trying to peer in through the glass window. He went back to the bell and kept his finger there. But no-one came.

And then he realised that of course Timson had gone home to his lunch. Of course he hadn't answered. He had probably finished the job. If he wasn't he'd be back later on.

And possibly, he thought impatiently, the old man didn't so much as know when Rachel would be back. So what was the point in coming back? He'd call round that evening he told himself. If Rachel was back, good. He'd question her about Deeford and they'd set his curiosity at rest, talking it over. If she wasn't back—there was always Wednesday.

•　　•　　•

It was simply because he had to go back to the café to pay the bill he had ignored in his sudden rush out, that he rang Timson. He saw the phone beside the cash register, while he was apologising to the little Chinese woman, and saw the sign that said the phone could be used for calls at sixpence a time.

He said lightly, "I'll have sixpennyworth if you don't mind, Mrs. Wing," and she laughed and nodded, accepting the coin and then moving away.

He had thought in that sudden moment that if Timson was home at lunch he'd be available on the phone and he could ring and find out, perhaps definitely, when Rachel would be back.

But the old man sounded disgruntled and annoyed and he wasn't helpful at all. He bawled, so loudly that Stephen held the receiver away from his wincing body, "How should I know? Think I'm young women's keeper, do you?" He gave a shrill bray of laughter. "My old lady'd have something to say if I started keeping tabs on young women, now wouldn't she?"

"I just thought you might know," Stephen said lamely. "I'm sorry if I broke into your lunch, but I thought you might have finished in Miss Penghill's and wouldn't be back there this afternoon."

186

"Finished? Lord above, I never even started." With relish the old man went on, "You ought to see my list—tiles off, trees down, guttering broke, windows busted—I could keep going day and night for a fortnight."

"I thought you were in there this morning," Stephen broke in sharply. "Mrs. Wing said you were in there hammering."

"That I wasn't." The annoyance was back in the old voice. "Woman's hearing things. Women always are. Do a bit of hammering and they're at you, 'Can't you be a bit quieter, Mr. Timson—baby's sleeping'—as though a man can hammer quietly. Women don't think, that's their trouble. They don't . . ."

Stephen wasn't listening. He was holding the mouthpiece to his chest, saying to the little Chinese woman, "Are you sure there was hammering in there this morning?" and knowing only when he saw her startled look that there was urgency, even panic, in his voice.

"Yes," she nodded, making a fist on the counter, "bang, bang, bang." She smiled at him half doubtfully.

"Mr. Timson," Stephen was back at the phone, breaking into the old man's complaints, "there was someone in there hammering this morning. Mrs. Wing's sure of it."

"Do you think I don't know where I was?" the question was bawled. "Haven't been inside the place. Left a note yesterday first thing to say I would be coming. If there's hammering must be Miss Penghill herself." He added hurriedly. "Now don't tell me the lass's started trying to do the job herself. Worsen it she will!" He sounded in a temper. "Women've got no head for carpentry. Worsen things is all she'll do. Those steps're bad—nasty. Tried 'em yesterday when I took up her milk for her and when I trod . . ."

"*You* took the milk in?" Stephen looked blankly into space. "You mean she was there and you spoke . . ."

"Never did. I never said so, did I? Said I took the milk in.

187

She was gone then. I had to turn off a light she'd forgotten into the bargain. Women're . . ."

Gone, he thought in amazement. Gone, before the milk came. When? At five probably. And gone with a light left burning.

He spoke his amazement into the phone, knowing there was sharp urgency, a hint of panic, in his voice. And then he started to laugh. Because the old man was saying, "What're you getting ants in your pants about, man? Spent the night at her brother's she did. Rushed off there in a panic-paddy after that business of the baby sitter and prowler. Rushed away and . . ."

He went on talking and Stephen stood there, feeling a fool, listening to the old voice saying that of course Rachel was spending the nights with Deidre and Roger, to hold Deidre's hand. She'd only returned to the shop that morning, probably, to fiddle with some little job. The old voice was sharp with anxiety as it wondered if the job was the stairs.

But Stephen wasn't listening. He was apologising for troubling the old man, smiling at Mrs. Wing's anxious face, nodding to her and then going out into the sunlight.

$$\bullet \qquad \bullet \qquad \bullet$$

It was nearly three o'clock, when sharply, searing through the words of the conversation he was holding at the radio station, he thought of the dog, and the drawn curtains.

Curtains, he thought, and stopped in the middle of what he had been saying. Curtains drawn in the blaze of mid-day sunshine. And a dog unfed. How was it possible that Rachel had gone back to the shop that morning and had worked there, with the curtains drawn. And gone away again without feeding the dog?

And if it hadn't been her at the shop, what had the hammering been?

$$\bullet \qquad \bullet \qquad \bullet$$

Ann was alone when he went to the back door of the Penghill

house. She was seated on the edge of the kitchen table, swinging her plump legs, eating cake. She looked startled when he loomed up against the flyscreen of the door, then she smiled.

But he didn't smile back. He said to her, even as she was unlatching the door to him, "Is your Aunt here, Ann?"

She shook her head, surprise in her eyes.

"Where is she then?" he pressed.

"Dunno. Have some cake?" she invited. "Mummy's gone over to Mrs. Clancy's . . ."

"Ann," he knew his voice was sharp, "has your Aunt been here, sleeping here, since Sunday. Since . . ."

"No," she broke in, then asked eagerly, "Have you heard about any more prowlers like Sandy's. She was . . ."

"Ann," he took her arm, gave her a gentle shake, "please listen. When did you see Rachel last?"

"Sunday."

"After the prowler came? Did Sandy ring her up? Did she come over then?"

"Oh no. She went before that."

"Did anyone from here ring her up and tell her all about things?" he pressed.

"No."

"She didn't ring you up, after my session. I spoke about Sandy's prowler in that, Ann. Did Rachel ring up then and ask you all about it?"

She shook her head. "I guess maybe she didn't listen," she volunteered abruptly. "I guess maybe she had a visitor and was talking."

"A visitor? At that hour? Who was it?"

"Dunno," she moved a little away from him, her eyes wide and surprised. "Someone rang up for her and I said she'd gone and they asked her new address. I don't know who it was."

Panic was suddenly there, unleashed. His thoughts were a confusion of drawn curtains, an unfed dog, a voice in the night asking for Rachel's address, Deeford with long scratches on his face, Rachel asking Sandy about a golden-haired man and Rachel and Ann . . .

He said sharply, "Ann, you and Rachel were in the reserve on Sunday, weren't you?"

Her cheeks suddenly reddened. She backed against the sink, watching him, her small mouth tightening, then she said shortly, "Mummy said I wasn't to talk about that. Not to anyone."

And it wasn't important, he thought. Nothing was important now except the one imperative question — where was Rachel?

. . .

Mrs. Timson had given him a list of names. He'd found the old man at the second of the addresses and at first had met only with stubbornness. He didn't have the key on him, Timson had protested heatedly. And there was guttering right in front of him half fixed. He wasn't going to leave it.

"You can get it," Stephen told him savagely, "or I get the police to force you to do it."

In offended silence they went back to the Timson house and drove back to Provence Street. Stephen remained silent through the whole journey. He knew that if he was wrong he was going to be a laughing-stock. Timson would relish telling the story to anyone who'd listen. He didn't care. Let the world laugh. So long as Rachel was safe nothing else mattered. If she was safe already maybe she'd laugh at him too. Maybe she wouldn't. Maybe she'd let him admit he'd been a fool too long, and forgive him and throw everything away that she had and go with him.

They went into the shop, still in silence. It had a closed, shuttered smell, and there was only quietness. Timson didn't look at the younger man. He went hurrying to the stairs, dropped to his knees, and then said triumphantly, "Never been touched."

But Stephen was brushing past him, running up the stairs, searching through the small neat room, and coming down again. He was halfway down the stairs again when he saw it and remembered Giddings saying, "I thought he might have done a smash and grab . . . he was talking about a vault they say . . ."

He had to force himself to cross to it and try the door. It held fast and he started to knock on the door. Urgently. Six knocks and then silence. He paid no attention to the old man, to the excited questionings. He simply went on knocking.

And then faintly, into the silence, there was a single knock from inside the vault.